Little Mark Underground

Patrick McGuire

Illustrated by
Julia Ilushin

Copyright © 2025 by Patrick McGuire

All rights reserved.

No part of this book may be reproduced in any form or by any electronic or mechanical means, including information storage and retrieval systems, without written permission from the author, except for the use of brief quotations in a book review.

Softcover ISBN: 978-1-7387073-2-4

E-Book ISBN: 978-1-7387073-0-0

First Edition

Contents

Chapter 1   1
Banished to the Garden

Chapter 2   7
An Unexpected Encounter

Chapter 3   15
Pizza Boxes and TV Screens

Chapter 4   21
The Corridors of Doors

Chapter 5   31
The Computer Mines

Chapter 6   37
The Tower of Admin

Chapter 7   45
Cowboy Roy and the Power Plant

Chapter 8   53
Doctor Freedrake and the Neo-Capacitor

Chapter 9   61
An Unexpected Visit

Chapter 10   71
Ruby the Giant Worm

Chapter 11   77
The Yellow-Green Grasslands

Chapter 12   85
The Town Centre Dance Party

Chapter 13   95
A Giant Eats Himself

Chapter 14   101
A New Giant is Born

Chapter 15   107
Faeries are Real

Chapter 16   113
How to get to the Land Beyond Imagination

Chapter 17 *The Cemetery of Ex-Pets*	117
Chapter 18 *The Secret Garden*	127
Chapter 19 *A Race around the Seasons*	135
Chapter 20 *Don't Forget to Follow your Feet*	143
Chapter 21 *Our Favourite Show*	147
About the Author	150

for all my teachers great and small

Chapter One

Banished to the Garden

Little Mark didn't like being called Little Mark, but everyone called him that because he always seemed to be the littlest one in the room. His parents were bigger. All his brothers and sisters were bigger. Practically everyone in the whole neighbourhood was bigger, except for little Emily next door, but she was still a baby and couldn't even walk on two legs.

Today was Sunday and everyone was angry at Little Mark. He had slept late, and then, while everyone was waiting to go to church, he had trouble getting ready. First, he put his shirt on back to front, and then he got toothpaste all over his clip-on tie. He was almost ready until he put his shoes on the wrong feet and tripped on his way out the door. His mother became exasperated as she changed his shoes to the correct feet and accused him of making mistakes on purpose and not wanting to go to church. That's when Little Mark made his biggest mistake of the whole day. He admitted that he didn't want to go to church. Church was hot and stuffy and boring, and he never understood what was going on.

"Opinions? From a little boy who doesn't even know how to tie his shoes?" said his Mom.

She hopped with up and down with anger and pulled him out to the car by the scruff of his neck like a momma cat carrying her kittens, telling his brothers and sisters what a bad boy he'd been. They expressed the shock and annoyance required to keep the attention away from themselves, and his father began to lecture them all on the importance of church. All his brothers and sisters stuck their tongues out at Little Mark when his parents weren't looking. Little Mark felt bad about what he had said, but he wasn't sure why.

They arrived at church, late as always, and his mom and dad sat on each side of him to make sure he paid attention and didn't get into any more trouble. He soon became sleepy, and his head would nod slowly to the side, and his parents would nudge him awake with a disapproving look. Their looks were a sure sign that he would be in big trouble as soon as he got home. When church finished, they pulled him by the arm to the family minivan, lecturing him on his lack of respect for everything and everybody, including things that he didn't even know anything about because he was still too little to understand. His brothers and sisters followed behind smiling, knowing that they couldn't get in trouble if their parents were busy scolding Little Mark.

"You'd better be a good boy when we get to Auntie Mabel's," his mom said, "Or you won't be allowed to leave your room for a week."

"Auntie Mabel's house is even more boring than church," thought Little Mark, but he had learned his lesson. He would never say his opinion out loud no matter how true it might be.

There was nothing to do at Auntie Mabel's house except listen to the grownups talk about grown up things. Auntie Mabel served nothing to drink except watery milk, and nothing to eat except the kind of cookies that didn't have any sugar in them at all. They might as well have been eating dried bread, thought Little Mark, another opinion that he kept to himself.

When they got to Auntie Mabel's, they had to walk through her garden. There wasn't much grass to play on in the garden — definitely not enough room for a proper game of tag or hide and seek. There were only flowers and trees, and odd little statues of dwarves, and bugs, and beavers, and faeries. The inside of Auntie Mabel's house smelled like flowers too — the dry, dead ones that always made Little Mark sneeze. Auntie Mabel had two dogs, both poodles, who were so old that they had faded into each other. Tara and Sky, once distinctly chocolate and grey, had both turned into a faded, yellowy, beige. They had started like opposites and were now more alike than different. They both had terrible, stinky breath, and slobbered and licked and jumped on Little Mark as soon as they saw him. There was never any place for Little Mark to run away from them because Auntie Mabel's place was so small and so stuffed with furniture.

Auntie Mabel collected knick-knacks. She had all sorts of little animals made of glass, fragile porcelain dolls, bowls of dead flowers, candles, and the robed men that Little Mark remembered from church. Her most special statues were of rosy-cheeked children climbing trees, carrying baskets or jumping fences — the kind of kids that you find in old children's books and faerie tales that don't look anything like the kids that you see in real life nowadays.

Auntie Mabel displayed her figurines next to her dining room table on two tall glass shelves. She always showed them to the kids, each time telling them how many dollars each figurine was worth, just like she had the time before. The kids were never as impressed by the figurines as their Auntie, mostly because they weren't allowed to play with them or even touch them at all.

Toys you can't even play with? Little Mark thought that was an awful idea, but kept that opinion to himself as well. Auntie Mabel loved her little statues of kids more than real-life boys and girls. Today, however, Auntie Mabel had a special surprise for all the children. She had bought a computer.

All Little Mark's brothers and sisters were so excited when she told them. They laughed and danced with joy and then began playing computer games in the next room. Little Mark wanted to join too, but his mother and father said that he had been such a bad boy that he would have to sit with the grownups at the dining room table and drink watery milk while they talked about important grown up things. There would be no fun for Little Mark today.

Little Mark looked so glum that Auntie Mabel gave him extra sugarless cookies to dip into his watery milk. Little Mark smiled when he got them and said thank you because he knew he would get into more trouble if he did not. He quietly took his seat next to the glass shelves full of Auntie Mabel's prized statues and ate his sugarless cookies and drank his watery milk, listening to the grownups speak about important things that were of no interest at all. Sometimes he would sniffle because the smell of the dried flowers tickled his nose and then his mother would shoot him an angry look. His nose began to itch and tickle more, but he became determined to hold in his sniffles to avoid getting into even more trouble.

Tara thought the sugarless cookies were treats and began begging next to Little Mark. He didn't want them himself so, when no one was looking, he tossed his last cookie to her. Sky saw Tara with a cookie and jumped up on Little Mark to get one too. Little Mark didn't have any cookies left so he leaned back in his chair to get away from Sky. Both dogs jumped on him and pushed him into his large glass of watery milk which spilt all over the table and onto his mother, his father, and his Auntie Mabel.

His mother and father jumped up, yelling. Tara and Sky yelped and licked at the spilled milk, and Little Mark lost track of his sniffles. Astonishingly, the itchiness of the dead flowers shot all the way up his nose to his eyeballs and, before he knew it, a tremendous sneeze flew out of him with ferocious intensity, sending him hurtling backwards through the air. He flew backwards into the two glass towers of figurines that were soon crashing to the floor all around him. All the statues smashed into little, tiny bits, spreading glass all over the floor, causing panic in the room. Auntie Mabel cried, the dogs yelped, and all his brothers and sisters laughed and laughed with delight, even though they knew that they shouldn't.

Everyone was unharmed, but his mother yelled at him loudly and picked him up and carried him outside onto the small patch of grass in the middle of Auntie Mabel's garden.

"You will stay out here for the rest of the day," she yelled, and she slammed the door.

Little Mark was stuck in the garden and looked inside from the outside, watching his brothers and sisters play while the grownups cleaned up and tried desperately to piece together all the broken figurines.

Chapter Two

An Unexpected Encounter

"Why did they send me out here?" thought Little Mark, "It wasn't my fault that the glass shelves came falling down. It was Tara and Sky. They jumped on me, and I didn't have any cookies to give them."

Little Mark didn't like being in Auntie Mabel's house, but not being allowed in was worse. He wasn't allowed to listen to the boring grown-up talk and watch his brothers and sisters play computer games, so that is exactly what he wanted to do.

Instead, he had to just sit on the little patch of grass in Auntie Mabel's garden all by himself with no one to talk to. He couldn't understand what he had done wrong. Sometimes he just said what was on his mind, but mostly, it was just bad luck. His circumstances were a result of his circumstances, and he didn't know what to do to get allowed back inside, or what to do while he waited. What if they didn't love him anymore and never came out to get him?

Maybe he would be out there forever.

He began to sniff the air outside. At least the flowers outside were alive — not like the dead ones inside that had made him sneeze. The garden wasn't so bad really, though he couldn't stop thinking about being left out there all alone. He was sad and decided to sulk and cry, and when nobody listened, he sulked and he cried some more. Then, when nobody came, he started to look around.

In the garden there were ferns and flowers and trees — all things lush, green and growing. There were also statues. The outside statues were much bigger than the figurines inside. A tall woman in a long dress, was in the centre with a basket of wheat, looking down at the birdbath below her. Tiny birds would flit by, and drink from the water, taking a bath at her feet. Little Mark looked at her bashfully, like she was real.

In the flower beds around her were painted statues of toy donkeys pulling carts, of cartoon bees and rabbits, of gnomes or dwarves or elves, who most often only lived in faerie books. One garden gnome at his feet, had a little green cap, and curly green shoes, a bushy red-brown beard and a round, red nose the shape of a strawberry.

Little Mark thought it looked really funny and very lifelike, so he reached down and gave the nose a squeeze.

"Hey! Watch where you're touching," said the gnome to an astonished Little Mark, "How'd you like it if I squeezed your nose?"

"You can talk?" exclaimed the startled Little Mark.

"Wow," said the gnome, "You're a regular detective."

"But you're not real. You can't talk."

"I'm plenty real and I got no problem talking. It's just that most people don't listen. I'm kinda surprised that you can hear me. Most people like you just pretend they can't and call it the wind or something. Maybe you're one of them special kids."

"Hmm, special? I am a little more special than I'd like to be today," said Little Mark thinking about all his troubles, "They stuck me out here because I've been bad and everyone else is inside having fun."

"So, you're out here having, what? The time of your life?"

"Well, I'm having something," he said, "But I didn't know that dwarves could talk."

"Dwarf? You're calling me a dwarf? You people upstairs don't know nothing. Is it a dwarf, a goblin, pixie, a sprite? No! I'm a gnome. Some people are so ignorant. What you call me says more about you than me, kid."

"Well, what is your name, Mister Gnome?"

"Oooo, Mister?" said the Gnome, "Now you're so formal. You can call me Phil. That's what most people call me."

"Well, hi there Phil, my name's Mark or Little Mark, like most people call me."

"You don't look so little to me," said Phil the Gnome, who had to look up at Little Mark even though he was just a little boy, "If you were a gnome, you'd be a giant. But then if you were a giant, you'd be a very tiny one."

"Well, I'm not a tiny giant or a giant dwarf," said Little Mark, "I'm just a boy and a little one, or so I hear. Tell me, do you live here in my Auntie Mabel's garden?"

"Sometimes," he said, "I usually live downstairs, but sometimes I gotta come up here to work."

"Work?"

"Yeah. I'm up here planting mushrooms."

"Planting mushrooms?"

"Yeah, most of us garden creatures live downstairs. We only come up here for special occasions or to work."

"But what's downstairs?"

"Just my house and all my friends and well, all my enemies too. There's lots of stuff actually. I think the brochure says lands of wonder and kingdoms of magic – a couple of kingdoms anyway at least. Truth is, I don't even know the half of it. You could spend a few lifetimes down there and not even get to the bottom of it all. The dirt goes pretty deep, you know."

"You live in the dirt?"

"Listen to this guy, I tell him about kingdoms, and he calls it dirt. Are we speaking the same language, kid?"

"You said dirt," said Little Mark, "All I was doing was repeating what you were saying."

"Oh," said Phil the Gnome, "You're a repeater. That's not particularly promising. If you want to live downstairs, you better have something to say. How do you get anything new if you only repeat what you hear?"

"I'm more than just a repeater," said Little Mark, "I'm only little but I think my own thoughts, but I don't usually say them out loud because that gets me in trouble. I have all sorts of ideas about all sorts of things – even things I don't understand. And there are so many things I don't understand. I'm still just so little."

"Well, I'm littler than you and there's only one way to understand what's standing under you," said Phil the Gnome, "You should come down there with me?"

"Down there? Down where?"

"Downstairs. To the underground."

"Uh, I don't know," said Little Mark. "That sounds a little scary."

"Well, if you want to be the kind of guy who understands stuff, then you're gonna have to take these kinds of plunges."

"Umm... I don't know."

"You gonna spend your whole life never knowing?"

"Umm... uh... I don't know," said Little Mark.

"Yeah, I know, you said that already. It's like, your favourite saying."

"Well, I want to go. But do I have to go forever? Can I come back?"

Little Mark Underground

"You can always come back, kid," said Phil the Gnome, "It ain't always easy, but you can come back. And time works different down there. It don't count for folks like you. You'll be back in no time, no matter how long you stay down there."

"Is it dangerous?"

"It probably won't kill ya, if that's what you're worried about."

Little Mark wasn't sure what he should be worried about.

"Umm," said Little Mark, "Should I ask my parents?"

"Yeah, of course, go and tell them that you are going to go to some sort of underworld with Phil the Gnome and see what they have to say about that. Maybe they'll let you out of the house again when you are, like, fifty. This ain't no amusement park, kid. This ain't no field trip from school. There ain't no permission slips. It's the chance of a lifetime to see something that most people don't ever get to see. Are you coming, or aren't you?"

Little Mark thought about it for a while. He couldn't imagine going because he had no idea about where he was going. But then, he also could not imagine not going. Would he really go through life having met a real live gnome and not having learned everything about the place that he came from? Did he really want to spend his whole life wondering? Really, how could he turn down a trip like this? His family wouldn't care anyway. His parents probably wouldn't even miss him. They would probably be happy he was gone. One of his brothers or sisters could have all the attention.

"Okay, I'll do it," said Little Mark.

"Okay," said Phil the Gnome, "But don't blame me if it ain't all it's cracked up to be."

"So, how do we get there?" said Little Mark.

"It's the mushrooms," said Phil the Gnome.

Little Mark looked down at the mushroom that grew at his

feet while he had been talking to Phil. He reached down and picked it up and was just about to pop it into his mouth when Phil the Gnome jumped up and knocked it out of his hand.

"What are you doing, kid? Are you crazy? Sheesh! That mushroom will kill ya if you eat it."

"But you said..."

"I never said eat the mushroom, kid," said Phil the Gnome and he pulled out a pouch from his belt, "It's the mushroom dust that does it – that's the stuff that makes the mushrooms grow."

Phil the Gnome put a pinch from his pouch in his palm and blew. Where the sparkles floated to the earth, a hole opened up at their feet and he stood at the edge.

"You coming, kid?" asked Phil the Gnome with a wink as he jumped.

Little Mark hesitated and looked around. There was no one there. He shrugged his shoulders, and then he jumped.

The hole closed behind him and Little Mark was gone.

Chapter Three

Pizza Boxes and TV Screens

Little Mark wasn't falling but he did have a kind of momentum. He glided behind Phil the Gnome like the dirt was air and he was riding a root through the earth. He heard himself yelling but he wasn't afraid. After quite some time, he landed with a thud in front of a doorway that was in an underground hallway of red clay soil.

"We're here," said Phil the Gnome.
"Where's here?" asked Little Mark.
"My house," said Phil the Gnome, "You coming in?"
"Sure," said Little Mark.
He opened the door and Little Mark followed him in.
"Sorry about the mess, kid, but my cleaning lady hasn't come in, like, six years, and it's usually so dark that I don't have to look at the place."
"Well, where's the light switch?" asked Little Mark.
"I don't need lights," said Phil the Gnome, "I'm a gnome. I can see in the dark. It's one of the bonuses of my little package."
"Then why's it so bright in here right now?" asked Little Mark, "Why can I see?"

"That's you kid. You glow," he explained, "You surface guys come down here sparkling your little lights off. Apparently, you are special. The dark is too dark for you guys, so you glow. You don't even know what darkness is. You surface people are all glitter. Down here, we learn to see in the dark, but you just get rid of the darkness altogether with your natural glittering."

"You mean I don't need a flashlight down here?"

"Your glittering will get you by, kid."

It was true. He was glowing. He was astonished to look at himself and see a light coming from within him. His hands, his arms, his whole body was shining. Down here, he was no ordinary boy — he was a glower. He glowed. He illuminated the world around him.

His glowing showed a shocking scene. Phil the Gnome's apartment was even smaller than Auntie Mabel's and even more stuffed with stuff. He didn't have knickknacks and figurines though. He had pizza boxes. All the brown clay furniture and every clay countertop was covered with pizza boxes and disposable food containers. The dining room table was full, the coffee tables were full, the kitchen, couches and bathrooms, were all full. In fact, there weren't too many places in the whole apartment where wasn't a pizza box or empty carton. Phil moved some pizza boxes off the top of his easy chair, plunked himself down, leaned back, and put his feet up to watch television.

"You eat a lot of pizza," said Little Mark.

"You are what you eat," said Phil the Gnome proudly, "So, statistically speaking, I am 93% pizza."

Little Mark moved a stack of pizza boxes too and took a seat on a brown clay couch next to him. He was much bigger than Phil the Gnome and took up all the space on the couch, crouching down so he wouldn't hit his head on the low ceiling.

They watched the gnome version of prime time television. It began with game shows and reality TV and then an hour's worth of gnome sitcoms. Little Mark was fascinated at first, until he realized that all the stories were the same as the shows upstairs at home, except that all the actors were gnomes. Phil watched avidly while Little Mark lost interest. He tried to interrupt a few times, but each time Phil the Gnome gave him a shush.

The evening went by in thirty and sixty minute time-slots, and after a few more hours of shows, the news came on. Little Mark finally felt it was a good idea to ask Phil the Gnome some questions.

"So, um, Mr Phil," asked Little Mark, "Now that I'm all the way down here, what are we going to do?"

"I don't know about you, but I'm gonna watch the next show. It's gonna be a great one."

"But you brought me all the way down here and we are just going to watch television?"

"What else are you gonna do? Besides, I didn't bring you down here. You came down here yourself. You know that thing they call free will? Well, you got it, kid. I didn't kidnap you or nothing. What do you want – a guide or something?"

"A guide? Yes, I would like one very much," said Little Mark.

"Okay, I'm a guide," said Phil the Gnome, "This is my living room. Ain't it glamorous?"

"But that wasn't what I was looking for."

"Oh, you wanted what you were looking for?" said Phil the Gnome, "You should have mentioned that. What is it that you are looking for?"

"I don't know."

"So, you want what you are looking for and don't know what that is and you want me to figure that out for you."

"I guess so," said Little Mark, "I was kind of hoping you could show me around a little bit. Could I see some of those kingdoms of wonder or something? The guides in all the stories my mom reads to me guide people around and stuff."

"This ain't no story, kid, this is real life and it's only a kingdom for the king. It's just regular life for everyone else. Welcome to the underworld."

"But the rabbit in Alice and Wonder..."

"I ain't no rabbit, kid. And this ain't no Wonderland. This ain't no book. It's real life. Does this look like some sort of kingdom of magic to you?"

"I don't know. I've only seen your apartment, but this can't be everything," said Little Mark, "There's gotta be more."

"Oh, there's more, kid," said Phil the Gnome, "There's lots more, but you gotta figure it out for yourself."

A look of disappointment came over Little Mark and he suddenly just wanted to go home.

"Then how do I get back home?" he asked.

"There's lots of ways back," said Phil the Gnome, "But mostly it just happens naturally, when your glow wears off. See, it's wearing off already. That always seems to happen when people come by to visit me. Stick around here, kid, and your glow will be gone in no time. Then you'll be back in your auntie's garden waiting for mommy."

"But if I do go, Phil, where should I go?"

"You start by opening the door and following your feet."

"Thanks for all the advice," said Little Mark, trying to sound as sarcastic as he could. Why did Phil the Gnome change so suddenly?

"Don't mention it, kid, I got you to where you're going. You can thank me later."

"I'd thank you now if you gave me a reason to thank you."

"Yeah, go tell it to the rabbit," said Phil the Gnome.

Little Mark let the door slam quietly behind him.

Phil the Gnome sat back down in his easy chair, flipped channels and thought about ordering a pizza.

"What a star," he said out loud, "It is gonna be a great new show."

Chapter Four

The Corridors of Doors

The outside of Phil the Gnome's home was a dark place indeed. The only light was Little Mark's glow. He thought about Auntie Mabel's garden, about going right home, but he didn't know the way. Phil the Gnome had said if the glowing stopped, he would go home automatically, but was that really true? Maybe he would just be stuck alone in a dark, strange place. He hoped for something around the next corner, anything really, a surprise — maybe one of those lands of wonder or something.

The path at his feet was paved with bricks of red and the walls were a red-brown clay. Little Mark marched forward and turned a corner, but found nothing. He turned another. There was nothing there either. He turned another and another and another, and the same thing happened. He turned so many corners that he didn't know where he was or where he was going. After a time, he gave up hope of finding anything around any more corners and stopped. He began to look at his own hands as their glow began to fade, and the inside of the cave around him began to get darker. That made him afraid. It really would get dark if he stopped glowing.

He didn't notice the buzzing until it was all he could hear. He wondered what it was. He wasn't sure if he should be happy or scared. At least it was something. He moved forward to meet it, but as it got louder and louder, he became more and more nervous. Maybe a surprise would not be such a great thing after all. Maybe there were worse things than the dark.

Suddenly, right before him, just inches away from his face, was a giant insect as big as his whole head. Little Mark turned to run, but he hadn't even taken two steps before the insect was directly in front of him again. He ran the other direction, but the insect was in front again, too. He turned many times, but each time he ended up looking at the bug in the face until he became dizzy from all the spinning. Finally, he stopped and stared the bug in the face. It had big, bulbous eyes like a fly, a long pointy nose like a mosquito, and two antennae that moved in every different direction. Its wings moved so fast that it looked like they weren't even there, the bug hovering in front of him like a hummingbird.

"Where are you going?" it asked in a raspy, whining, buzzy voice.

"I don't know," said Little Mark nervously.

"Then how will you know when you get there?" asked the insect.

"I don't know," said Little Mark.

"You don't know very much, do you?"

"No, I don't," said Little Mark, "I only just got here."

"Where's here?" asked the insect.

"I don't know."

"Let me see," said the insect, "You don't know where you are, you don't know where you are going, and you don't know what it will look like when you get there. Do you know who you are? Do you even know that?"

"I'm a boy. I'm just a little boy and I don't know where I am, and I don't know where I'm going, and now, I'm talking to a giant bug who won't let me escape. This is really scary."

Little Mark didn't know what to do so he just sat down on the ground and cried.

"Don't cry, little boy," said the insect, "What's your name?"

"It's Little Mark."

"You don't look so little. You're about ten times the size of me."

"Where I come from, things like you are about a thousand times smaller than me and people are still scared of them."

"Well, you don't have to be scared of me, Little Mark," said the insect, "I might look scary, but looks can be deceiving. I couldn't even hurt a fly. I am here to help."

"Okay, well, that's good," said Little Mark, "Because you do look scary."

"One person's scary is another person's beautiful so I will take that as a compliment. As for you, Little Mark, considering your obvious glow, I think you must be from upstairs. How did you get down here?"

"Phil the Gnome brought me here from my Auntie Mabel's garden."

"Phil is no gnome," said the insect, "He is a goblin if I've ever seen one. If you met him, you are lucky there's a you left of you."

"Phil the Gnome seemed nice to me at first," said Little Mark, "But then once I got down here, all he did was sit there and watch TV."

"You're lucky that's all that he did," said the insect, "These gnomes are always up to no good. Don't you know that kids shouldn't go walking around with strangers?"

"But he wasn't a stranger. He was a gnome. How often can you meet a real live gnome?"

"About as often as you look for one if that's what you want," said the bug, "They're as common as rats and donkey's tails. Do you think running away with him is a good idea just because he's different?"

"I wasn't running away — I was running towards, and I am pretty sure all of us are different kinds of different," said Little Mark, "You especially. You might be the most different of them all. I've never even heard of a giant, talking bug before."

"Well, I am definitely different from Phil the Gnome," said the insect, "My name is Bill. I'm a full service bug. I know where everything is down here and I can take you wherever you want to go."

Little Mark was nervous but Bill seemed great, even if he did kind of hum all the time. His voice buzzed from his antennae, but his whole body hummed even when he wasn't speaking.

"What kind of bug are you anyway?" asked Little Mark.

"I'm a Bill the Bug," he said, "And I am one of a kind."

"You're not like any bug where I'm from," said Little Mark, "Bugs can't fly in the ground upstairs."

"But that is exactly what I'm doing right now. So, you see, what is impossible from your perspective happens all the time down here. Therefore, you must change your perspective. People where you're from have no idea what happens below their own feet, or even in the air in front of them. Bugs do lots of things that most people don't know anything about at all."

"Like what?"

"Well, I, myself, see everything but don't really say anything. I let everyone else do that," said Bill the Bug, "I can see things from all angles but I'm what they call objective. I don't pick sides, though I do choose where to point my head.

Right now, I am pointing it at you! It is my job to say hello to anyone from upstairs who visits down here. I'm like the welcoming committee. It's not every day that we get someone from up there, down here. It is a truly special day for everybody. Isn't that right everybody?"

Bill the Bug paused for dramatic effect like there was an audience.

"Who are you talking to?" asked Little Mark, looking around. There didn't seem to be anyone else except the two of them.

"Take a closer look," said Bill the Bug, and he whirred up to Little Mark, looking closely at him with his big, bulbous eyes. Little Mark realized that each inch of the eyes were covered with thousands of tiny, smaller eyes all winking and blinking and watching from different angles and spots. Little Mark was looking thousands of eyes in the eye.

"I'm talking to my eyes," said Bill the Bug.

"That's so creepy," said Little Mark.

"You think it's creepy seeing all the eyes," said Bill the Bug, "Imagine trying to be them. All of them. They're always changing their perspectives. So many eyes make it so difficult to see."

"I'm glad I've only got two," said Little Mark.

Maybe his guide was a little unusual, but after meeting Bill the Bug, Little Mark finally felt the adventure beginning. Now he wondered where to go. That's when Bill the Bug buzzed in with his big idea.

"Since you haven't been anywhere, I'll take you to the place where it all begins. I will take you to the source."

"Where's that?" asked Little Mark excitedly.

"The best way to know is if I show it to you and to do that, you have to follow me!"

Bill the Bug took off like a shot, zooming ahead through the corridors. Little Mark ran after, but lost him before he even started. He ran along the red brick road, past so many doors, and came to an intersection with even more identical doors in every direction.

He called out. Where had his guide gone? He became sad. He wasn't even good at following.

Suddenly, Bill the Bug came whizzing back from around a corner, spinning and looping and yelling, "Follow Me! Follow Me!"

Little Mark caught his breath and chased as fast as he could. They ran past countless corridors full of doors going off in each direction.

Bill the Bug slowed down to let Little Mark catch up.

"Do you know where all these tunnels go?" asked Little Mark.

"Of course," said Bill the Bug.

"But there aren't any signs?" said Little Mark.

"It's my job to know everything," said Bill the Bug.

"Where are we?" asked Little Mark.

"These are the Corridors of Doors. This is where everyone lives — anyone who's anyone, that is."

"Isn't everyone someone?"

"Yes, everyone is someone, so I suppose anyone is someone too. It's a manner of speaking. This is where the people live."

"All the places look the same here," said Little Mark, looking at all the identical doorways that looked like every other doorway.

"I know. We gave them all a choice to live any way they wanted, and they chose what everyone else did. It didn't matter who or what they were, they wanted the same thing, although they wanted more of it than all the others."

"More of what?" asked Little Mark.

"More of the same," said Bill the Bug.

Little Mark, himself, began to get bug-eyed after they passed so many doors.

As they walked along, they came across a donkey pulling a cart behind him. It was just the same as a small statue in Auntie Mabel's garden. Little Mark asked about it.

"You'll notice a lot of things from upstairs down here," said Bill the Bug, "Everything that happens here, happens up there as well — even if you guys don't know it. I'm surprised you never saw me upstairs, though my greatest talent is not being seen."

Little Mark said hello to the donkey, but the donkey just ignored him and kept pulling his cart, stacked high with brown boxes. Little Mark became frustrated because the donkeys were busy delivering, and not paying attention to the people around them.

"They're ignoring me," said Little Mark.

"Donkeys don't talk, silly. They just deliver."

"What do they deliver?"

"Everything."

"Everything like what?"

"Everything like all the things in the mines."

"Which mines?"

"That's where I'm taking you," said Bill the Bug, "The mines are the source of everything."

The last corridor opened up into a wide, tall cavern as big as a whole city. The cavern was full of forests of giant stone ice cream cones, hanging from the ceiling, or coming up from the floor. Red brick roads wound through the Stone Forest from the Corridors of Doors to the back of the cavern. On all the roads coming and going, donkeys were pulling carts full of brown boxes. Little Mark noticed that all the carts were coming from the same place.

"What's that?" asked Little Mark, pointing at the hole at the far end of the caves.

"That's where we're going," said Bill the Bug, "That's where everything comes from. Those are the Computer Mines."

Chapter Five

The Computer Mines

The steady rhythm of hoof hitting brick, in line after line of donkeys, had Little Mark dodging and jumping behind the roadside stalagmites lest he be mistakenly crushed by an inattentive hoof. The donkeys were pulling cart after cart of stacked boxes along the red brick roads that wound through the stone forests of the caverns. Bill the Bug hovered above, answering the curious little boy's questions.

"What's in all the boxes?" asked Little Mark.

"Stuff," said Bill the Bug.

"What kind of stuff?" asked Little Mark.

"Stuff for down here, stuff for upstairs — every bit of stuff for every little place, all come from those mines."

"Everything?" asked Little Mark.

"Every noun you know — the places, the things, even the people are manufactured there, really. Everything for everywhere comes from in there."

"Even people?" asked Little Mark.

"Well, you are what you eat, so to speak," said Bill the Bug, "And the people behind those doors consume a lot of stuff from the Computer Mines. Everything that people could even think of wanting comes from in there and that makes them who they are. Some say that the people are the final product of the mines."

Little Mark was surprised at the size of the operation. The donkeys moved a lot of boxes. Slow and steady, the donkeys would plod with their heads down, carrying boxes to all the doors in the corridors where they would be opened and emptied by the creatures inside, some of whom were donkeys themselves. There was a variety of creatures inside those doors, but despite any differences, they all emptied boxes — many, many boxes.

As Bill the Bug and Little Mark got closer, Little Mark became impressed by the size of the mines. It had to be the biggest hole in the whole world.

"That is where we turn the world into stuff," said Bill the Bug proudly.

As the donkeys continued to plod forward, however, Little Mark noticed something wrong with their carts. They were all empty. The donkeys were pulling carts full of nothing. It was line upon line of plodding donkeys with empty carts going round and round in a loop.

"That's strange," said Bill the Bug, "The donkey carts are always full."

They hurried their way through the donkey lines to the mouth of the mines and came to a large gate with a big button on it which said, "Press here."

Bill the Bug pressed the button with his long mosquito nose and a large screen popped up from under the ground and began to play a movie. It was a video introduction to the mines narrated by a large Beaver-Mole with a white hardhat and flashlight forehead.

"That's Lou," said Bill the Bug, "He's in charge down here. He'll tell us what's going on."

The video was a pre-recorded tour of the world below the down below world, that they were already in. The video told them about the state-of-the-art diggers, conveyors, collators, assemblers, boxers, packagers, and other strange machines made to make everything that Little Mark had ever seen before, and a great many more things that he hadn't.

"Welcome to the Computer Mines," said Lou the Beaver-Mole in a radio announcer's voice, "Birthplace to the Future."

The video promoted the products of the Computer Mines by taking Lou the Beaver-Mole on an exciting, rollercoaster ride throughout the mines.

Little Mark was impressed to watch such an amazing promotional video and wanted to see inside the Computer Mines himself, but the gate remained closed.

"Why are the carts empty?" said Bill the Bug, "We've got to talk to Lou. He's usually here to welcome people but he might have been automated. They're removing people from the system these days — people are a big problem for the system."

They knocked and knocked for quite some time, until Lou the Beaver-Mole finally did poke his head out the door, wiggling his nose and squinting suspiciously. He wore a white hardhat and forehead flashlight, which he shined into their eyes. Lou looked so much bigger on TV. When they heard him talk, they were even more surprised. It wasn't the radio voice from the video at all.

"G'day folks," said Lou the Beaver-Mole, "What can I do for ya?"

He shone his headlamp closely into the eyes of Bill the Bug, looking with his blind, beady eyes, and recognizing him with a buck-toothed smile. Then, he looked closely at Little Mark, inspecting him the same way, before he got a surprised look on his face. It was like he recognized Little Mark. He was about to say something, when Bill the Bug interrupted him.

"Hi Lou," said Bill the Bug, "The new kid and I came here to have a tour of the mines but we noticed that all the carts are going out empty."

"Yeah, we can't fill 'em up anymore," said Lou the Beaver-Mole.

"What?" asked Bill the Bug, "Are all the mines empty?"

"No, well, there's still lots of stuff in there, eh, but we don't have the power to get it out."

They did a walking tour of the mines which were pitch dark, except for Little Mark's glowing and Lou the Beaver-Mole's forehead lamp. All the robots were ready to work, the conveyer belts were all ready to convey, the machines were all ready to machinate, but there was nothing moving.

"What's the matter," asked Bill the Bug.

"Well, ya know, I come to work and do my job and everything should work just fine but then, like, the machine just stops workin', eh. It just stops movin' and that's it, ya know. I tried to fix it, but it isn't broke. It's just the system. It would work if there was power, but there's just no power and just too much stuff."

"Well, what are we going to do?" asked Bill the Bug alarmed.

"Well, I still gotta work, ya know, gotta make a living, I can't change the whole system myself, ya know. They shoulda listened ta me when they were making it, eh, but they didn't. Now they got a big mess, and they don't even know it. So, I guess I'll just keep it going until they figure it out."

"I'm not sure if that's such a good idea," interrupted Little Mark, who had been listening quietly, "Why don't you solve the problem?"

"What do you know, Mr. Glow? I've been working here a

long time and that's how these things work," said Lou the Beaver-Mole, getting upset, "I just work with the system that they gave me. I didn't make it. Why don't you try workin' for a change? It's hard work just keeping it going, eh."

Lou the Beaver-Mole kept mumbling to himself about why he wasn't doing anything about the problem.

"He looked so good in the movie," said Little Mark sadly, "But it wasn't even his own voice."

"Everyone looks better in the movies," said Bill the Bug, "I think it's just good editing."

They realized they weren't getting anywhere so they left.

"This may be the source," said Bill the Bug, "But it isn't where they make the decisions. We have to visit the Tower of Admin."

Chapter Six

The Tower of Admin

The Tower of Admin reached high up to the top of the cavern past the Computer Mines. Its two-way mirrored glass reflected the outside back on itself, while the inside got a shaded view of the world around. Out front, they came to a set of doors, a blinding light flashed into their eyes, and a mechanical voice said, "Temporary Access Approved."

The doors opened automatically.

The high-ceilinged room had grey walls and a single steel desk with a receptionist, who was guarding an elevator door behind him. The receptionist was a parrot, a giant one, with bright, multi-coloured plumage. At least that was what Little Mark imagined the body of the parrot looked like because it was covered by the greyest suit that anyone could imagine. If white reflects light and black absorbs it, the receptionist's suit denied that any light even existed. He looked at them across a great number of silent telephones.

"Yes?" asked the Grey-Suited Parrot, straightening up his grey tie.

"I'd like to inform you that the Computer Mines have stopped working," said Bill the Bug.

"Oh, I'm sure you are quite mistaken, sir," said the Grey-Suited Parrot immediately, "Everything is working at full capacity, and there are absolutely no problems with the system. We've actually been experiencing a significant amount of growth above our projected surpluses in productivity."

"Yes, but we've just come from the mines, and they are definitely not working," said Bill the Bug, "There's nothing going out on the donkeys' backs."

"Yes, you must be mistaken, sir," said the receptionist. "According to reports, productivity in the mines is on the increase. I'd like to get your name, as you are an unofficial person, and we can't have unofficial people making unsubstantiated reports that are unconfirmed. I'll make an official report about you to the proper authorities."

"Most people know me. My name is Bill, Bill the Bug, and I am actually a friend of You-Know-Who."

"Oh? You know You-Know-Who?" said the now nervous Grey-Suited Parrot receptionist, "Umm... you should have stated that earlier. I'm going to have to talk to my superior."

The Grey-Suited Parrot made a call and explained the situation. After much discussion, the single elevator behind him opened up, and Little Mark and Bill the Bug were ushered upstairs.

The elevator went up one floor, and they entered a vast room of cubicles and desks. Each desk in each cubicle had a unique, Grey-Suited Parrot in an identical grey suit, sitting at its desk, staring into a computer screen and talking on the phone. One Grey-Suited Parrot led them through the crowd of cubicles, and into an office at the back. There was another Grey-Suited Parrot, this one wearing a yellow tie and sitting behind a desk reading a newspaper.

"Yes?" she asked, as she used her claw to push her glasses up her beak to get a closer look at them.

They told her that the Computer Mines weren't working.

"I'm sorry but you must be mistaken," she replied, "The organization is working at full capacity. Our productivity is increasing, and our growth will continue exponentially."

Little Mark and Bill the Bug told her what they had seen with their own eyes, but she disbelieved them until Bill the Bug mentioned that they were friends of "You-Know-Who," who Little Mark didn't actually know, but Bill the Bug at least said that he did. The Grey-Suited Parrot in the yellow tie quickly became flustered and then helpful, and they were brought back to the single elevator where they went one more level up, through another office full of Grey-Suited Parrots staring into their computers in cubicles, to an office at the back, where they talked to the manager of the next level who, himself, was wearing a blue tie. He also disbelieved them until they mentioned again that they knew "You-Know-Who." He became flummoxed, and then helpful enough to bring them up to the next level where the same story was repeated.

Each Grey-Suited Manager Parrot at each level was dressed identically to the manager of the previous level, except for a colour-coded tie. Yellow, blue, white, brown, black, purple, and pink – the ties of each level were all different colours, but the Grey-Suited Parrots were the same, whatever their level. They each denied the problem, some showing elaborate figures and charts, maintaining that the organization was experiencing unparalleled growth and prosperity. They didn't believe what Little Mark and Bill the Bug had seen with their own eyes. They believed the charts they had made themselves instead.

At one point, in front of a Grey-Suited Parrot in a red tie, Little Mark became exasperated and blurted out, "Nothing is moving!"

The Grey-Suited Parrot in the red tie paused to glare at the little boy and said, "You must be mistaken. I've been analyzing the forecast and cross-referencing with other very large charts, and productivity is at near full capacity."

"Look out your window. Can't you see? It is right there before your eyes."

"Preposterous, my silly, young man," said the Grey-Suited Parrot with the red tie, "The system is perfect as long as we don't do anything to change it."

Little Mark and Bill the Bug were frustrated and again mentioned that they knew the mysterious, "You-Know-Who," and the Grey-Suited Parrot in the red tie ushered them up to the top floor of the Tower of Admin.

The offices at the top floor of the Tower of Admin were quieter than the other levels and the pace of staring into the computer screens went at a much more leisurely speed. Instead of the multi-coloured Grey-Suited Parrots, the top floor of the Tower of Admin was reserved for the Ivory-Coloured Cockatoos who also wore grey-coloured suits and red ties. The Ivory-Coloured Cockatoos were bigger than the other parrots and payed even less attention to Little Mark and Bill the Bug. After waiting patiently at the desk, they were finally led to a back office with a Grey-Suited Ivory-Coloured Cockatoo sitting behind a large, steel desk. The walls of his office were made of glass and overlooked the Computer Mines and roads of donkeys pulling empty carts.

"Yes," said the Grey-Suited Ivory-Coloured Cockatoo, looking up from behind a pair of reading glasses, "What brings you here?"

"Well, sir, we've been down to the Computer Mines, and nothing seems to be moving," said Bill the Bug.

"Impossible," he said. The Grey-Suited Ivory-Coloured

Cockatoo pulled out some binoculars to look down at the mines.

"Yes, it would seem that what you are saying looks to be true, but our eyes can be deceiving. The question is actually debatable. I don't think we should jump to any conclusions."

"But you are sending out nothing," said Little Mark, "The machines have all stopped working. The whole system is stopping, and you aren't doing anything about it. It's your job. If you don't do it, then who will?"

"Actually, we are doing something about it. Look at all of the charts and graphs we've produced. They show that if we continue doing the same thing with confidence, the results will work out for us. We don't need your wild accusations to question our confidence. This is a very important situation — too important for people to know anything about. We must insist you keep your ideas to yourself."

"But people will notice," said Little Mark, "People aren't dumb. And people are going to have to make changes to solve the problems."

"Actually," said the Grey-Suited Ivory-Coloured Cockatoo, looking at his screen, "We seem to have gotten some reports that might correlate with your assumptions, and they have discovered who is to blame. It seems that the cause of the reduction in productivity is, in fact, Lou the Beaver-Mole."

There was silence.

Little Mark was dumfounded.

"We just talked to Lou the Beaver-Mole. He doesn't have any power. He can't send out all the boxes without any power. He wants to change the system, but he can't, so he just continues to work in the old way because he doesn't know a new one."

"You are mistaken, young man," said the Ivory-Coloured Cockatoo, "Every Parrot on every level of the Tower of Admin has just produced a report that says that Lou the Beaver-Mole is to blame."

"But we just talked to them and they just told us there wasn't even a problem at all."

"You asked them to change their opinion and they have," said the Ivory-Coloured Cockatoo, "They have all decided that the problem is Lou."

Little Mark started to argue, but Bill the Bug interrupted.

"Listen, I'm a friend of You-Know-Who," he said, as he winked half of his eyes, and the Grey-Suited Ivory-Coloured Cockatoo squawked loudly with surprise and delight.

"You know You-Know-Who?" he said, "I have actually talked to him once on the phone. Well, he never actually said anything, and hung up while I was talking, but do you think we should call him?"

"Yes, well, I think I should talk to him because you guys are wrong about Lou," said Bill the Bug.

"Could all of us really be wrong?" said the Grey-Suited Ivory-Coloured Cockatoo.

"Just make the call," said Bill the Bug.

The Grey-Suited Ivory-Coloured Cockatoo picked up a phone, dialed, and handed the phone to Bill the Bug.

"It's Bill," he said, "I'm at the Tower of Admin. I was just in the mines and nothing's moving. Oh, you know? Of course, you know. Yes. He's with me. How does it look from your side? Really? Yeah, we're close to there. Okay, we'll check it out."

"He wants to talk to you," said Bill the Bug, as he handed the phone back to the Grey-Suited Ivory-Coloured Cockatoo.

"Me?" said the Grey-Suited Ivory-Coloured Cockatoo excitedly, as he took the phone in his talon, "You-Know-Who wants to talk to me? I didn't think he even knew who I was!"

"We're leaving," said Bill the Bug to Little Mark, "You-Know-Who wants to talk to you too."

"I don't know who You-Know-Who even is. How does he know me?" asked Little Mark.

"He knows everything, including you," said Bill the Bug, "We'll be meeting him soon enough. We just have one other stop to make."

"Where are we going?" asked Little Mark.

"There's trouble at the Power Plant," said Bill the Bug, and they walked toward the elevator.

"I can't believe I got fired," they heard the Grey-Suited Ivory-Coloured Cockatoo say as he hung up the phone, "I only just did what I was told."

Chapter Seven

Cowboy Roy and the Power Plant

Little Mark and Bill the Bug continued down the red brick path as it wound around behind the Tower of Admin and through a forest of stalactites. Amongst them was a big, boxy building, a giant rectangular cube, without any windows. Its entrance was two swinging doors like the ones at an old western saloon, and above the door was a large sign that said, "POWER."

They pushed the doors open and inside the large waiting room was, indeed, a western saloon. Sitting alone at the long wooden bar, was a human-sized cowboy staring down at a drink as he mumbled to a robot bartender. Little Mark was getting used to being the biggest one in the room, so now a regular-sized cowboy seemed extra huge.

"Howdy," said the cowboy, who had a little glow like Little Mark's, "You guys the maintenance crew?"

"No," said Bill the Bug, "You-Know-Who sent us to find out what the trouble is."

"D'you know what I'd like to tell You-Know-Who to do?" said the Cowboy with a steely grin.

"Pardon?" said Bill the Bug.

"You-Know-Who has been sitting on his can, when this here old plant don't have any power left in it."

"He sent us," said Bill the Bug.

"Who are you and what are you going to do?"

"I'm Bill the Bug and this is Little Mark, and we're here to find the problem, and then report back to You-Know-Who."

"Little Mark, huh? You're from upstairs, ain't ya? I remember when I first came down here like you, all shiny new and glowing, just like this whole place used to be. Now the glow is gone from this place and the mine's going too," he said, stretching his faintly glowing arm out slowly to shake Little Mark's hand, "Pleased to meet ya, Little Mark. My name's Roy, and this here power plant is my land, but you are most welcome here. I don't know about the bug, but you're alright. You're my kind of people. I like my kind of people."

"Oh, he's a nice guy and has helped me quite a lot," said Little Mark, vouching for Bill the Bug.

"You know him very long?" he asked.

"Not really," said Little Mark.

"So, you don't really know him then, do ya?"

"He seems nice," said Little Mark, "He's showing me around."

"Oh, they got you trusting 'seems', do they?" said Cowboy Roy, "Good for them. Trusting 'seems' don't seem too smart to me."

"He's my only friend down here," said Little Mark.

"Life's rough when you don't know your friends," he said, "So you're here for the problem then? There ain't nothing you can do. When what's wrong ain't broken, you can't really fix it. It works like it's supposed to, but the situation is different now. They have to change the whole thing, but that's not gonna happen."

"Well, what is the problem?" asked Little Mark.

"The problem ain't that the mine ain't working, and it ain't that the plant ain't working. It'd be working just fine if it had any power. The problem is that there ain't any power because your You-Know-Who ain't been sending us any rabbits. You know the power plant needs rabbits to survive. Since the donkey carts have all been empty, we ain't got a single one."

"Rabbits?" asked Little Mark.

"No Rabbits?" said Bill the Bug, shocked, "No wonder…"

"And the rabbits we do got," said Cowboy Roy, "The real ones that never ran away. They lost their taste for the carrots a long time ago."

"Carrots?" asked Little Mark.

"No carrots?" said Bill the Bug, "No wonder. We need to see the Capacitor."

"Oh, you wanna see the machine, do ya?" said Cowboy Roy, "You think you can do something? Well, be my guest."

Cowboy Roy led them through the swinging doors at the back of the saloon. It was a big room with the projection of a yellow-green field on one wall. In the middle of the room was a large mechanical merry-go-round contraption. In the centre was a tall, metal pole with arms sticking out from the top. Each arm had a chain dangling from it, and on the end of each chain was a carrot. The rabbits were clamped to an arm from the bottom of the centre pole, a steel lock wrapped around their cotton tails. The carrots dangled just out of the reach of each rabbit, and they would hop to get a taste of the carrot, making the Capacitor turn with each hop. They hopped and jumped for the carrot, but rarely caught one. The Capacitor spun, though most of the chains were now dangling freely, and the responsibility to make the machine turn depended on just two rabbits.

"My god," said Bill the Bug, "The Capacitator is spinning

so slowly. It should be whirring along like a bee. This is what sends the energy out to every home, to every place down here."

"There ain't no rabbits comin' these days," said Cowboy Roy, "There used to be thousands and now we only got Flopsy and Mopsy here. It's emergency power now and blackouts in all the Corridors of Doors."

"But the rabbits were famous for multiplying," said Bill the Bug, "There are always more rabbits coming,"

"Not these rabbits," said Cowboy Roy, "You-Know-Who decided to switch to the new ones that come from the Computer Mines just like everything else, and now we don't have the power to get more rabbits out of the mines. The old multiplying ones have all run off, so all we have are these two, to send out a little power just to keep the old stuff running. When old Flopsy and Mopsy finally kick it, I don't know what we're gonna do. We won't be sending no power nowhere. Then the Corridors are gonna get real dark."

Around the corner came the two bunnies who were making the circuit that made the whole thing move. Flopsy and Mopsy hopped tiredly, a metal lock around each bunny's cotton tail, and in front of each bunny on a chain, was a carrot. Each time the rabbit jumped for the carrot, the chain behind it tightened and pulled the Capacitator forward, swinging the carrot out of its reach. Flopsy and Mopsy looked thin and tired and sore.

"Stop it," yelled Little Mark, "You're hurting them."

"We're not hurting them," said Cowboy Roy, "They love it. We're giving them hope. They can't help themselves. Hopping is their favourite thing to do."

"But you're hurting their tails."

"No," said Cowboy Roy, "They love to jump."

"But they never get the carrot," said Little Mark.

"Oh, we make sure to give them a little taste every once in a while so they remember why they're hopping, but we can't give them too much or they don't stay hungry. What do you want to do? Stop the whole system just because you think that a couple of rabbits look tired?"

Little Mark was sad. He wanted to set Flopsy and Mopsy free, but they were working so hard and were so important to everyone. He was skeptical about whether Flopsy and Mopsy really wanted to be there.

They went back into the saloon and Cowboy Roy sat down at the bar and poured himself a drink. Then he began to get sad.

"I remember a time when this saloon was full. Folks from upstairs, folks from downstairs, everyone used to come down here when times were good. Now it's just me. It looks like the end of the line. I remember when I came down here for the first time. It seems so long ago now, and everything was so bright. I glowed, the cave was bright and green, and we made this place great. We built the corridors, the caverns, the tower, the plant, and the mines. We made this place what it is. Now the place is faded, smokey, and dark, and our whole way of doing things looks like it's ending. I don't know how we got here. I don't know what went wrong. I look at you, Little Mark, and I see me, before I made this place. I see the future I had once. It all seems to be behind me now. The power is leaving the plant."

As he was talking, Cowboy Roy's glow got fainter, and then he himself began to fade. He was turning into a ghost before their eyes. He took one more drink, looking sadly into his glass, and then up at Little Mark. Then he faded into darkness, disappearing into nothing.

Little Mark was shocked. Bill the Bug was shocked. There was nothing left but an empty stool. They both remained quiet for several moments.

"This is serious," said Bill the Bug, "It's time to go see You-Know-Who."

Little Mark looked at the empty stool and wondered if he might be next.

* * *

"Who is You-Know-Who, and why doesn't anyone ever say his name?" demanded Little Mark, as they walked up the steep, steel steps on the side of the cavern. "I want to know what this world is all about. What goes on here? Where are we going?"

"So many questions. It's difficult to know which one to answer," said Bill the Bug, "'You-Know-Who is one name for a man who has many. He sounds scary but he's not — to his friends. People call him You-Know-Who because everyone knows who he is. He is this place, and this place is him. He built it all – the mines, the towers, the doorways, the roads. It's all his work. Cowboy Roy likes to take the credit, but You-Know-Who did it all and everyone knows it. People used to call him many things, but he put a stop to that. Now he's just You-Know-Who around here, mostly because there wouldn't be a here, here without him."

"But who is he?" asked Little Mark.

"He has titles and names — Doctor, sir, Freedrake or Malahat, but none of those names capture who he is, so people just call him You-Know-Who."

"Where does he live?"

"Look up ahead."

The steel steps reached their way up to the top of the cavern where, blended into the side wall, were two giant doors. Little Mark couldn't imagine what was behind them, but whatever it was, was big.

"He's like a wise man on the hill," said Bill the Bug, "He makes the plans and creates his inventions and they come down to us like they have always been there."

"What does he make?"

"He makes everything for everybody. He makes their jobs, makes their products, makes their lives, gives them purpose. Some say he's from upstairs, but he doesn't glow like you. Doctor Freedrake made the Computer Mines and trained the Beaver-Moles to dig. When they started to find the marvels that lay down below, he created the new systems – all the robots and conveyors. He made everything work. He made the Beaver-Moles into foremen, built the Towers of Admin, and put all the donkeys to work, but I think his biggest achievement was creating power. He made the Power Plant and learned to use the rabbits, and now it all works by itself just as long as we press the right buttons."

Little Mark became excited and nervous to meet such an important person.

Chapter Eight

Doctor Freedrake and the Neo-Capacitator

The doors to Freedrake's castle made Little Mark feel small. They towered high above and creaked and rumbled open automatically as soon as they arrived. On the plush, red carpet in front of them was a tiny, white mouse dressed in a tuxedo and standing up on his two back legs.

"Gut evening," said the White Mouse, "Velcome to zee home und laboratories of Doctor Freedrake Malahat, also known as Zee Doctor, or Freedrake, or Malahat, or as zhey like to call him from vere you are coming – You-Know-Who. Please be szo kind as to follow me."

He escorted them down the carpet and into the entrance chamber. On the walls were hundreds of video screens showing what was happening throughout all Freedrake's lands. Little Mark was mesmerized by all the images on the screens, many showing the places he had been. On some of the screens, Little Mark saw himself walking down the carpet, and that made him feel strange.

The room was lavishly furnished with red velvet couches

and gold trim like a proper castle. There were large life-sized photos of nature and trees between the screens. In a large red and gold high-backed chair was a tall man with wild, white hair, and a white flowing beard. He wore a crooked business necktie over a white, collared shirt, but instead of a business suit, he wore a white lab coat. He had a kind but stern smile on his face. This was You-Know-Who — Doctor Freedrake Malahat.

"Welcome, my most esteemed colleague," he said in a commanding voice to Little Mark, "I've been waiting for you to come."

Malahat stood up, ignored Bill the Bug, and reached out to shake Little Mark's hand. Little Mark glowed brightly when he shook the hand of someone so obviously important.

"You must be tired from your journey. We can sit here and rest, or I can give you a tour of my most humble home."

"I'm not tired at all," said Little Mark, "I'd love for you to show me around."

"Well, of course, my good young man," said Doctor Freedrake, "I'll have Fritz make us up some refreshing beverages before we walk through the laboratories."

The white mouse in the tuxedo scurried through a small door and came back carrying a tray with blue drinks, which he served to Freedrake and Little Mark. Bill the Bug landed at Freedrake's feet and nestled there like a pet, as a fireplace appeared next to them, lighting itself and warming the room. It became quite a cozy scene.

"This is where I watch my creations," began Doctor Freedrake, "Throughout the lands, I need to know what is going on. I need to see that all is working to plan. As you can see, my home is my work, and my work is my home. In fact, this whole habitat is my creation, and it does not end at the walls of this house. My world, so to speak, is my creation. My world is my work."

The blue drink was sweet and tasty and Little Mark drank deeply as he listened.

"In my lands, we bring order," he continued, "We want to make sure that everyone has their place and gets everything that they need. Everything needs to work here, just like everyone must work. It is what the whole land is for. It gives us purpose. As long as the system is in place, the place becomes perfection."

"But what about the donkeys?" asked Bill the Bug, "They're empty. What are we going to do about them?"

"Please do not interrupt," said Malahat impatiently, "I'm talking to our very important guest, and I don't want him to worry about trivial things that can easily be solved if we make the right decisions. Come Mr. Mark, I must show you our work."

They walked toward the wall full of screens that opened up like curtains as they neared. They stepped through and into the laboratories.

The laboratories were filled with beakers and tubes, dripping chemicals, and bubbling potions. There were gears grinding and machines moving – tubes and wires, bolts and screws. There were experiments of light, of sight, of sound, and colour – big experiments, little experiments, and in-between-sized ones — all being carried out by a busy staff of white rats wearing white lab coats, ignoring completely Doctor Freedrake and Little Mark and Bill the Bug, as they walked through. Little Mark asked questions and Malahat answered with words that were too big for Little Mark to understand.

After some time, however, Bill the Bug became impatient. He had come to the laboratories for a reason, and he hated being ignored.

"Doctor, Doctor," he interrupted finally, "What about the rabbits at the Power Plant and the Computer Mines. The empty boxes are piling up everywhere. What are we going to do about that?"

Freedrake looked at his interrupter, irritated.

"Yes, my dear bug, you are correct. That is our most pressing problem and that is, in fact, why you and our young friend are here. We, together, will be the ones to solve the problem."

"We?" said Little Mark, "What can I do to help with the problem?"

"My young friend, you are the most important part," said Freedrake Malahat. "You are helping right now just by coming here, and you, will be the one who helps the most because you, my young man, are the future."

"What?" asked Little Mark, "But how?"

"Let me show you something," said Malahat as he unveiled a velvet curtain with a machine behind it, "You see, the problem right now is not really with the rabbits. They are much the same as they have always been. The problem is the carrots. Right now, there just are not enough carrots to go around, so not enough rabbits get enough of a taste often enough to make them want to jump. The carrots themselves don't taste as good as they used to either, so a lot of the rabbits have run away to eat grass, of all things. No carrots, means no rabbits to pull the Capacitator. If the Capacitator doesn't move, we have no power. No power, and everything stops."

"So, what are we going to do?" asked Bill the Bug excitedly.

"Well, my dear bug," said Malahat, "All the creatures create such problems, and it is left up to science, and myself, to fix them. The situation has set me off creating my latest inventions. You see, I have been studying the glow that surface dwellers get when they come down here. There is energy in this glow. There is power in this glow. There is enough power in this glow to power everything, both down here, and most things up there as well. I have therefore created a new machine that can do just that. Behold! The Neo-Capacitator!"

He dramatically pulled back the curtain and behind, they saw a steel machine with buttons and dials and lights that were not yet lit.

"You are going to get surface people to come down here to make that machine move?" asked Little Mark.

"Not just any surface dwellers," said Freedrake Malahat, "You! You are going to make this world glow just like you do. You are going to save the world!"

"How will I do that?" he said, "I don't like carrots, and I don't want a chain tied to my tail. I don't even have a tail."

"Forget the carrots. All you have to do is be natural, be yourself. Do what you love. Do what you do. Glow!"

"All you want me to do is stand here and glow?"

"Yes, that is great, but actually, the more you move, the more you glow, and the more fun you have, the better. Do what everyone loves – dance. It would be best if you danced."

"Dance?"

"Yes, dance."

"But what if I don't want to dance?"

"Oh, but I forgot the most important part," said Doctor Freedrake Malahat, "The catalyst."

He pressed a button and big stereo speakers appeared from the floor. The room started to shake with a heavy bass and strong, thumping, throbbing music. Little Mark wasn't sure he wanted to dance, but there was something infectious about the music. He began to move his feet and his body, shaking it like a washing machine on the spin cycle. Freedrake joined along, and so did Bill the Bug. Soon, all the white rats in the lab coats all took notice, and began to dance as well. The whole room began to take on a bright glow. The Neo-Capacitator began to whir into operation, powered by the glowing dancer. Little Mark could not see it, but his dancing and his glow spread through the Neo-Capacitator and into all the machines throughout Doctor Freedrake Malahat's lands. From the Computer Mines to the Corridors of Doors and Tower of Admin, all things began to move into action again.

Chapter Nine

An Unexpected Visit

So it was that Little Mark danced. Each morning, he would sit with Doctor Malahat as Fritz, the mouse in the white tuxedo, would bring them a big, sugary breakfast as they discussed the matters of the world. Doctor Malahat would describe the experiments he was doing and the machines he was making, and they would watch all the screens together – watching all the donkeys pulling, the gnomes and beaver-moles digging, and the grey-suited parrots producing very, very large charts. Most importantly, everyone was opening so very many packages. Each morning, Malahat would tell Little Mark about how the world worked.

"The land is made to be used," he would tell Little Mark, "And we are made to use it. We have made many products, but our most important product is people. We have made a way for people to find their place. People are happy when they know who they are, and what to do, and we tell them what that is."

They finished their breakfast and happily went off to do their work. Little Mark would go into the laboratory, press play on the machine, the music would start, and he would move himself in time with it. He danced all day every day and through most of the night, as Fritz or Bill or Doctor Malahat himself, would bring him refreshments and dance along. Little Mark loved the dancing, not just because of the music, but also because he felt useful. He was saving the kingdom.

This became the greatest time for all of Freedrake's kingdom. The mines were being dug like they never had been before, and more and more new things were being made for more and more people to put in their homes, and the power plant was running at full capacity. All of this was because of Little Mark's dancing, and he loved to dance. He danced by himself. He danced with Bill the Bug. He danced with the white rat lab technicians. But, he loved it most when Freedrake himself, if he wasn't too busy, would dance along with him. Little Mark glowed the brightest, and the Neo-Capacitator worked its hardest, when he danced with Freedrake, because that is when Little Mark was happiest. Things were better for him down there than they ever were for him upstairs with his real family, he thought. This was his new family. That feeling went on for a very long time, until it stopped all of the sudden with an unexpected visit.

Little Mark was dancing by himself late one evening, glowing brightly as he practiced some steps that he was going to do with the lab rats the next day. The lights were going off all around him, but he hardly noticed.

Then, Phil the Gnome appeared out of nowhere.

"What are you doing, kid?" he said.

When Little Mark saw Phil the Gnome, he stopped dancing.

"What does it look like I'm doing?" he asked.

"Dancing," said Phil the Gnome.

"Exactly," said Little Mark, "But why should you care?"

"I always care about you, kid. You're like my little brother – my big, stupid, little brother."

"Stupid?" said Little Mark angrily, "Who are you calling stupid?"

"Why are you dancing, kid?"

"It's fun, I like the music, and I'm saving the world," said Little Mark.

"What world are you saving?" asked Phil the Gnome.

"The whole world down here," said Little Mark, "and some of the world upstairs too."

"You look at your little finger and you call it the world," said Phil the Gnome, "Is that what they call modern education?"

"People have been so nice to me. Not like you. You're just like everyone upstairs. You didn't care. You just took me down here and then watched TV."

"Yeah, you're right," said Phil the Gnome, "I coulda taken you down here and held your hand and showed you every place, but then you wouldn'ta found out for yourself. When you figure stuff out for yourself, it makes you feel better, and you remember it forever. You woulda seen my world, not yours."

"Yeah well, I did figure it out for myself, and I do feel better about it – no thanks to you. I needed your help, and you didn't do it. Bill the Bug and Doctor Freedrake helped me, but you didn't. Look at all the fun I'm having now, and you didn't even lift a little finger."

"Yeah, dancing by yourself in an armpit of the world while your friends suck your life away. Woo hoo – looks like paradise."

"I like it here," said Little Mark.

"You like it here because you don't know any better."

"I might not know any better, but I do know worse. What

you did was worse. Here I have friends. Bill's my friend. Freedrake's my friend."

"Oh, Freedrake's your friend, is he?" asked Phil the Gnome, "Let's see how much he likes you if you stop dancing?"

"He'd like me just fine."

"Yeah right, kid, I'd like to see that," said Phil the Gnome.

"He'd be okay about it."

"Okay, then do it – stop dancing."

"But I like dancing."

"So do I," said Phil the Gnome, "It's one of my favourite things in the whole world. But you wouldn't like it if you had to do it."

So Little Mark stopped dancing and a few minutes later, Bill the Bug came in and Phil the Gnome disappeared into the shadows.

"What's up Little Man," said Bill the Bug, "Why'd you stop dancing?"

"I'm tired," said Little Mark, "I don't feel like it."

"Oh, don't be so gloomy," said Bill the Bug, "You'll feel better if you dance."

"Yeah, maybe," said Little Mark, "But you're not dancing either. Why don't you dance?"

"I can dance, sure. I'll dance with you if you want," and Bill the Bug started bopping up and down like a ping pong ball.

"You should dance alone," said Little Mark, "I want a break."

"But I don't glow when I dance. I don't make everything work. You need to dance."

"But you should dance just because you want to," said Little Mark, "Not because you want me to dance,".

"What are you? Some sort of temperamental artist? I always feel like dancing," said Bill the Bug, and he began to jump like a flea, smiling with a big grin on his face.

Little Mark just sat down and watched. After a while, Bill the Bug stopped dancing.

"Come on, Little Mark, you've got to start dancing or You-Know-Who will come and talk to you about it."

"Aha," said Phil the Gnome, stepping out from the shadows, "You don't have a choice about dancing. It's dance, or big trouble from You-Know-Who'."

Bill the Bug looked at Phil the Gnome with surprise.

"You've got a lot of nerve showing up here – goblin," said Bill the Bug.

"You've got a lot of nerve doing this to the kid, robot!" said Phil the Gnome.

"Robot?" said Little Mark.

"Bill the Bug here comes from the Computer Mines," said Phil the Gnome, "He's not even real. Nothing real comes out of the Computer Mines. Everything there is molded by Malahat into machines."

"Just because I'm a robot doesn't mean I'm not real. I am as real as anyone," said Bill the Bug.

"Really? You're more fake than anyone and not just because you're a robot," said Phil the Gnome, "You're the fakest friend anyone can have. You've been lying to Little Mark."

"I've always treated Little Mark well," said Bill the Bug.

"You've been taking advantage of Little Mark," said Phil the Gnome, "He has no idea what you're doing."

"He's enjoying himself," said Bill the Bug.

"Really?" said Phil, "Kid, look up at the screen over there."

He pointed at a bank of televisions that usually had pretty colours on them that Little Mark watched when he was dancing.

"I'm turning it to the big channel," said Phil the Gnome, and he cartwheeled over to the channel changer, and began pressing buttons.

"No, don't!" yelled Bill the Bug, and they began to wrestle over the controller. Phil the Gnome was able to toss the controller to Little Mark who changed the channel and saw... himself?

"It's not what you think," said Bill the Bug, "You make people happy."

"What's going on?" asked a confused Little Mark.

"You are the most popular channel on television, kid," said Phil the Gnome, "The most popular channel ever. You. People from all over tune in to see you do what you do. I don't know why, but they love you. They watch you dancing. They watch you resting. They watch you sleeping. They watch you watching them. They watch everything. The ratings are incredible."

"What do you mean?" asked Little Mark.

"The eyes of Bill are not really eyes," said Phil the Gnome, "They're cameras. The whole laboratory is full of cameras. The whole world is full of cameras. People all over the world just love to watch you walk, talk, dance, experience everything. Their watching you, makes the machine go even more than your glowing does. Sure, your glowing makes the system move, but making people watch is where the real power is. Every second of their watching feeds Malahat's machine, and they love to watch you. His machines feed on the energy of the watchers, and that feeds his machines. That's where the power comes from. Bill the Bug has been hanging cameras everywhere, and people have been watching you. You've made him powerful – you made them all powerful."

"Bill?" asked Little Mark, "Is this true? I thought you were my friend, and you were just using me?"

"It's not what you think," said Bill the Bug, "You're popular. People like to watch. They love you. You're famous."

"I didn't want that."

"I did it for you," said Bill the Bug.

"Did I ask you for that?" asked Little Mark.

"No."

"Well, no thank you," said Little Mark.

Bill the Bug paused for a moment, not sure what to say.

"It's too late for that," he said sadly, "It is one of those things you can't undo."

Just then, a door flung open, and in walked the Doctor. Phil the Gnome again disappeared into the shadows.

"What's happening, Little Mark?" asked Malahat, "How come you stopped dancing?"

"Why don't you just look on the screen?" said Little Mark.

"He knows about the show," said Bill the Bug.

"Oh that. That's no big thing. We did that to help," said Malahat, "We wanted people to like you."

"People I don't know?" asked Little Mark.

"Everybody," said Malahat.

"Why would I want everyone to like me?" asked Little Mark.

"It's better than having them hate you," said Malahat.

"I didn't want everyone to love me or hate me or even know me. All I wanted to do was to find something new."

"And he took advantage of you," said Phil the Gnome jumping out from the shadows again.

"What are you doing here?" said Malahat.

"I'm here helping a friend," said Phil the Gnome.

"So am I," said Malahat, turning to Little Mark, "I'm your friend, Little Mark. I take care of you."

"Yeah, he's your friend," said Phil the Gnome, "He takes advantage of you."

"That's not true," said Malahat, "I love Little Mark."

"Would you love him if he didn't dance?" asked Phil the Gnome.

"He loves dancing," said Malahat, "I dance with him sometimes. We all dance. It's what we do. Why don't you ignore the little goblin and dance for a while, Little Mark. It will make you feel better."

"I don't feel like it," said Little Mark.

"Come on, Little Mark," said Malahat, "Just a little dancing before dinner."

"He doesn't want to," said Phil the Gnome, "Why don't you ask him where the music comes from, Little Mark. It doesn't even come from here. Malahat doesn't have a musical bone in his body. He even steals the music."

"You shut up," said a furious Malahat, "You don't belong here, gnome. Boy – you dance, or you won't get any dinner."

"See! You just want him for the power he gives you – his dancing, his glowing, his whole life is what you want," said Phil the Gnome, "You don't care about him."

Little Mark looked at the angry doctor and knew that it was true.

"I want to go," he said.

"I'll get you out of here kid," said Phil the Gnome "There are better places than here. I'll take you to where the music comes from."

And before Malahat could grab him, he pulled out his pouch and blew a puff of mushroom dust onto the ground before them. They both jumped into the sparkling hole that grew at their feet and they were gone.

Chapter Ten

Ruby the Giant Worm

After a brief sensation of hurtling, they landed with a thud on a pile of dirt. Little Mark's first journey with Phil the Gnome had been smooth, but this one left them both lying in the dirt, dazed, until Phil the Gnome stood up and replaced his little green hat and dusted off his green-sleeved suit.

"These domestic flights are bumpy sometimes," he said.

"Where are we?" said Little Mark, brushing himself off as well.

"We're at the wall," said Phil the Gnome, "I wanted to go all the way through, but Malahat's got some sort of force field or something around the place, and the magic won't get us through the wall. You see, kid, Malahat wants to control everything to get everyone to do what he wants them to do. He is making the world into his world, by giving everyone what he tells them they want. Then he says his way is the only way and they've got to follow it, but he does it in a way that they think they're making the decisions themselves. Nobody even knows he's at war with them, so that's why he's winning. He's got all sorts of tricks and traps, but I'll get you outta here. Magic won't work here, so we gotta get through the old-fashioned way."

"Through a door?" asked Little Mark, "Which one?"

Little Mark looked up and down the wall and saw many doors in each direction to choose from. This wall didn't look like the edge of anything. It looked exactly like all the walls he had seen in the Corridors of Doors. There was nothing but doors in both directions as far as he could see.

"Doors only work if there's something on the other side," said Phil the Gnome, "Pick a door, kid. They're all the same."

Little Mark opened one of the doors and inside was a red brick wall all the way up to the top. He chose another door, and it was the same. He chose another, and another, and another, and they were all the same — one brick wall after another. These doors went nowhere.

"Malahat keeps the edge camouflaged," said Phil the Gnome, "He figures people won't want to go anywhere, if they don't think there is anywhere to go. They don't even know that there is a whole other world on the other side of this wall. The best way to keep people in, is to make them think there isn't any other place to go."

"What's on the other side of the wall?" asked Little Mark.

"That's for the folks who don't follow his rules — if they can get there. That's his brother's land."

"Freedrake has a brother?" asked Little Mark.

"Yeah, but they are about as different as oranges and onions. I think they're only brothers because they started out that way. They can't stand each other."

"Why?"

"Who knows? They're like oil and water. They just don't mix."

"How do we get there? What's the old-fashioned way?"

"Jeez kid, I forgot how many questions you ask," said Phil

the Gnome, "If we can't get over the wall, and we can't go through it, we're going to have to go under. I'm a digger, but I don't have my shovel right now, and even if I did, it would take weeks to get there that way. Malahat would catch us for sure, and then strap some chain to your tail like a rabbit, just to feed his machines. But I've still got a few tricks and a couple of friends. I'll get us outta here."

He reached into his coat pocket and pulled out a golden flute. He tapped it against the wall, and then put it up to his lips and began to play. It was a happy tune, and Phil the Gnome began to dance, leaping into the air and clicking his heels, his fingers flitting up and down the flute, his song getting louder and louder. Then, his fingers covered up all the holes and the sound of the flute hit its highest pitch. Phil the Gnome just held the note, letting it get louder, and louder, and louder — so loud that Little Mark had to put his fingers into his ears. Nothing happened at first, but Phil the Gnome kept on blowing, and soon they heard a loud, low, rumbling and shaking from below. It got louder, and louder, and louder too, and Little Mark got very afraid. Something was coming.

"Get out of the way!" yelled Phil the Gnome, and they both jumped and tumbled to the side, as the floor broke open between them and a large pile of dirt dumped on the ground at their feet. Then, poking its head out of the ground, was something even more scary indeed — the gaping mouth of a giant worm.

"You called?" it said.

"Yeah, Ruby," said Phil the Gnome, "We're trying to get to the other side."

"Sides? What are sides?" asked Ruby the Giant Worm, "I am a worm. We don't have sides. We only have dirt."

"I mean, we need to get to the other side of the wall," he

said, pointing to the red bricks beside them, "That's the direction you were coming from."

"You people are quite amusing," said Ruby the Giant Worm, "I live underground your underground. Everything you do is above my head. If the side you want is behind me, I assure you, it is much the same as here."

"Well, we can't stay here," said Phil the Gnome, "We gotta get this kid to the other side. He's the one who is supposed to change everything."

"Everything?" asked Ruby the Giant Worm, "You think people are everything? Dirt is everything. We're all just dirt in different forms. Everything begins and ends as dirt. And everything you eat does too. He might change people but he won't change dirt."

"People are changing the dirt a lot these days," said Phil the Gnome, "They're mining more and more of it into stuff. If we don't get him outta here, there might not be any dirt left for you to swim in."

"There's an ocean of dirt around us," said Ruby the Giant Worm, "The mine will eat itself before it ever gets all the dirt."

"There's no knowing what the mine might dig or how much of it," said Phil the Gnome, "And no place for us to go once they're done."

"If it's such a problem," said Ruby the Giant Worm, "Forget your sides and work on the dirt."

"Lovely idea," said Phil the Gnome, "But you don't have a mad scientist chasing after you."

"Alright," said Ruby the Giant Worm, "I'll take you where you need to go. I'm hungry, anyways. You should try some dirt. It's delicious."

"I dig the stuff," said Phil the Gnome, "But I don't eat it."

With that, Ruby the Giant Worm dove into the ground between them, taking a big mouthful of dirt, leaving behind a wormhole that was supposed to take them where they wanted to go.

"Let's go, kid," said Phil the Gnome as they entered the tunnel, "Sometimes the old-fashioned way works the best."

"What do you mean I'm supposed to change everything?" asked Little Mark, as he followed Phil the Gnome into the wormhole.

"Don't worry about it kid," said Phil the Gnome, "We'll get you to the other side and figure it out from there. You don't have to be anything but yourself and we'll be fine."

Chapter Eleven

The Yellow-Green Grasslands

Little Mark and Phil the Gnome entered the wormhole nervously. For all Little Mark's glowing, it was still a dark tunnel into an unknown place. Anything could be ahead of them, anything could be behind them, anything could happen. The dirt at their feet was soft and damp. It didn't seem safe. Little Mark asked Phil the Gnome if the tunnel could collapse.

"Definitely," said Phil the Gnome, "It doesn't usually happen right away, though, so, we're probably safe. If we're not, well, it will happen so quick that it won't matter anyway."

"Why did you tell me that?" said Little Mark, quickening his pace.

"Oh, you like lies better?" said Phil the Gnome, "Lies don't make you any safer."

"It would have made me feel safer," said Little Mark.

"Oh yeah, feeling safe. That's important." said Phil the Gnome, "Okay. The tunnel is safe. A tunnel collapsing is the least of your worries anyway."

"What should I be afraid of?" asked Little Mark.

"I can't tell you that," said Phil the Gnome, "You want to feel safe."

Little Mark wasn't sure if he was joking. They continued down the tunnel for a while longer and Little Mark got more impatient.

"When is this going to end?" he asked, "I can't imagine Ruby spending her whole life down here."

"This what Ruby lives for. The dirt, for her, is air," said Phil the Gnome, "It will go on just long enough to make you think that it's never going to end. And then it ends, but that's really just the beginning."

Little Mark was in the lead, getting stuck in the mud at every step. Globs of mud began dropping from the top of the tunnel, and they were full of bugs that crawled all over them.

"These bugs are driving me crazy," said Little Mark.

"Would you prefer the big robot bug you were hanging out with back there?" said Phil the Gnome.

Before he could answer, they heard a familiar buzz coming from behind.

"You'd better bet he'd like me better," said Bill the Bug, who whizzed in front of them, blocking the tunnel, "Little Mark remembers the good times we had together. We had fun, right Little Mark?"

He hovered ahead, smiling with his pointy nose and thousands of eyes.

"You had fun," said Phil the Gnome, "While Little Mark was working and making you guys rich. Remember?"

"Little Mark should come back to Freedrake's. We give him purpose."

"Little Mark doesn't need you for that," said Phil the Gnome, "He came down here to see new things and that's what he's gonna do."

Little Mark just kept walking as the Phil and Bill argued.

All he wanted to do was get to the end of the wormhole. It was dark and scary and could collapse at any time. He ignored them both and ran as fast as he could as soon as he saw the light.

* * *

The light seemed brighter because of the darkness they were leaving. They were at the base of the wall, and the world before them looked very, very different. As far as they could see were rolling grasslands basking in light. It was cavernous but bright. The wall on this side behind them, looked exactly like a regular wall — brick upon brick, as high as Little Mark could see. What startled him most, though, were the two bald-headed giants who loomed over him with arms folded, on either side of the unmistakable figure of Doctor Freedrake Malahat. He was dressed differently though, in long white robes instead of his usual white lab coat and tie.

"B-b-b-but I thought you were behind us," said Little Mark, catching his breath from having run so long in the dark tunnel.

"And yet here I am in front," said Malahat, "Why have you come here?"

"I wanted to get away," said Little Mark.

"Run away? From where? Your past? You bring that with you, wherever you go," he said.

"I wasn't running away," said Little Mark, "I was running towards. I wanted to come to a new place, and here you are. Why are you chasing me?"

"I chasing you? Really? I assure you, young man, I do not chase," he said, as the giants nodded along, "People come to see me if they can find me, but I don't chase them down. It would mean that I wanted something, and I assure you, I want nothing. Wanting things is the very problem with people."

"Everybody wants something," said Little Mark, "Don't they?"

"Do they?" he asked, "What do you want?"

"Hmmm," thought Little Mark, "I don't really know. It keeps changing."

"That's what wanting does. Right when you get it, it changes. What do you want, now that you are here, quickly, before you change your mind?"

"I just want everyone to get together and not fight," said Little Mark, "I want to see all the good and all the bad in everything, and then I want to see new worlds, discover new things. People say I'm a curious child. I love to learn new things."

"What if the other person is wrong?" said Malahat, "Shouldn't you fight them?"

"Who am I to know right and wrong?" said Little Mark, "I'm just a little boy."

"Oh, you are not just any little boy," he said, "And most children know what's right and wrong before they learn differently."

"Why would I want to fight you?" asked Little Mark.

"Why indeed?" he said, "You have nothing against me. You want everyone together in one place. That is what we do here."

The giants grunted in approval. Little Mark eyed them suspiciously. These giants were taller than trees, and he thought they might stop him and force him back into the Neo-Capacitor. The giants' faces smiled gently when they saw the fear on Little Mark's face.

"These are the giants, Bubbles and Stone," he said, "The giants join the dance of creation and make magic with us every day and every night. This is a land of freedom, where everyone is free to explore their wildest imagination and create a new future. Can you create a future or are you stuck in your past?"

"Well, I'm a little boy," said Little Mark, who was surprised by how different Malahat was now, "I may not know a lot, but I imagine that I've got a future of some sort at least. That's the one thing that all kids do have."

"You imagine?" said the old man thoughtfully, "Well, if you imagine, then you are in the right place. That is what we do here. We imagine. We can help you to imagine the kind of future you want."

"That sounds wonderful," said Little Mark, "You are so different now, Doctor Freedrake, I'm so excited that we can all get together and…"

And then he heard a voice coming from the wormhole behind him. He turned and was shocked. It was another Malahat — how could this be?

"If everyone is getting together, then I guess I am coming too," said the other Malahat.

"You are not allowed in here," said the Malahat that Little Mark had been talking to, "This is my land."

Phil the Gnome, who had been keeping quiet since they arrived, interrupted the situation to make formal introductions.

"This guy ain't actually Malahat, kid," said Phil the Gnome, "It's his brother, Weeblake. They're twins."

"But you said they were different," said Little Mark.

"They are," said Phil the Gnome, "They just look the same."

The brothers began to argue.

"No kings allowed here, brother," said Weeblake.

"I am no king," said Freedrake, "But you are. You are the prophet against profit, a false idol for the idle. You are the king of the slothful where the useless are free."

"Are you afraid of freedom?" asked Weeblake, "Afraid that all your subjects will run away like the rabbits?"

"We don't need those rabbits anymore," Freedrake said, "You can have them. I've solved that problem."

"Your solutions don't solve problems," said Weeblake, "Your solutions are the problem. If you solved everything, we wouldn't have anything left."

"Everyone gets everything they want because of me," said Freedrake.

"And they lose everything to get it," said Weeblake.

"We give people purpose," said Freedrake, "Everyone is useful and fulfilled."

"As long as they do what you say," said Weeblake.

"They have freedom because of me," said Freedrake, "We give them opportunity and they make what we all need. You make nothing in your land."

"Nothing is something," said Weeblake, "And we do much more than that. We make life. We make magic."

"You offer nothing, and call it magic," said Freedrake.

"You take everything away and call it freedom," said Weeblake.

Little Mark stood between the two brothers, the two twins, the two old men with their long, white, flowing beards and fiery eyes, unsure of what to do.

"Can't we all just be together?" said Little Mark, "I think we can do better if we work together."

Freedrake turned his attention to Little Mark.

"Please come back with me," said Freedrake, "I offer you an opportunity for a life of worth, of value, of purpose and productivity. You will help everyone to live and prosper. Do not squander your life here. We need you there."

"If your system needs a saviour," said Weeblake, "He might not be who you want."

It didn't make sense to Little Mark to have to choose, but he couldn't be in two places at once, so he had to. The brothers insisted he make a choice.

"Doctor Freedrake," said Little Mark, "I cannot go back

without seeing what is ahead. I would be very unhappy if I went back without knowing. I imagine my glow would disappear in no time, and then I'd be no good to you anyway."

"Don't waste your life," said Freedrake, "With me, you make a difference."

"The boy has made his choice," said Weeblake, "Now the wormhole is closing. You had best be getting back to your side."

Freedrake straightened his tie and adjusted his lab coat as he turned and disappeared into the wormhole, with Bill the Bug following closely behind, pausing to give Little Mark a sad look with his many eyes.

Weeblake clapped his hands, and the hole collapsed quickly. Little Mark looked at him with shock.

"Don't worry," said Weeblake, "He's my brother. He'll be fine, and you, my friend, are free."

He clapped his hands again and, in a flash, he disappeared, along with the two giants. Little Mark was left alone with Phil the Gnome in a wide-open grassland that had yellow-green grass as far as he could see.

"You made the right choice, kid," said Phil the Gnome.

Little Mark looked back at all the bricks in the wall behind him and hoped the gnome was right.

Chapter Twelve

The Town Centre Dance Party

The Yellow-Green Grasslands went on for as far and wide as they could see. The knee-length grass looked to Little Mark like the lawn of his family home when they got back from vacation. It was quiet, calm, and peaceful. The noise of the arguing brothers subsided into the swaying grass, echoing into memory on the wind. They began to feel the peace of the place as they walked away from the wall.

"It's all so natural here," said Little Mark, "I haven't seen a real plant for such a long time. I almost forgot that plants even smelled. There were many of pictures of plants at Freedrake's, but these plants are real."

"Sometimes you forget what you're missing till it is back," said Phil the Gnome, "You spent all that time with Malahat. He sure tricked you."

"I just followed my feet like you told me, and that is where they took me. Everything I did made perfect sense."

"A little too much sense," said Phil the Gnome, "It doesn't make sense to make sense all the time. It cuts down on possibilities."

"What was I supposed to do?" said Little Mark, "I didn't even know there was anywhere else to go. How are there possibilities, if I don't know what they are?"

"You got caught in the machine, kid," said Phil the Gnome, "That's the Bug's fault. He gave you all the information, so doing what he said made sense. That kinda sense will destroy everything. The wrong kind of sense does more damage than the thing it's supposed to fix. But we're here now. Here it's all about freedom. Now you can do whatever you want, however you want to do it."

As they wandered through the Yellow-Green Grasslands, they started seeing rabbits everywhere. They were all eating mouthful after mouthful of the yellow-green grass. The rabbits looked like the ones at Malahat's power plant, only healthier. One bunny hopped over and started sniffing at Little Mark's feet.

"They're the ones that got away," said Phil the Gnome.

"Got away?" asked Little Mark.

"Yeah," said Phil the Gnome, "Malahat had all the little bunnies tied up by the tail to the Capacitator in the Power Plant, making them all hop for the odd taste of carrot. Finally, they started to escape. You should have seen them when they first showed up. They were all thin and sick, until they could relax here, and eat the grass. The yellow-green grass is medicine for rabbits."

"They look healthy now," said Little Mark, reaching down to pet one.

Little Mark felt happy. His heart pumped in a way he hadn't felt in a long time. He felt the energy in his body, and decided to run. He ran for the sake of it, not to get away from anything, not to get anywhere. He ran to run. Phil the Gnome followed along, and pretty soon, all of the bunnies began to follow along as well. It was Little Mark and Phil the Gnome and bunny after bunny hopping along in a parade. Eventually, they became tired and flopped on their backs in the light, surrounded by bunnies who munched away on the soft grass. Then, they would get up and run some more, getting nowhere because there was nowhere to go. Little Mark loved the idea of not following anyone, but did wonder where they were going.

"Why do we have to go anywhere?" said Phil the Gnome. "The only destination is here, wherever it is, and we're here right now. Ain't it great."

They ran through the fields, the yellow-green grass whipping their shins. The sky was a yellowy twilight, that didn't come from any direction at all. Little Mark wondered where the light came from.

"I'm not sure where the light comes from," said Phil the Gnome, "They say that we build it with the magic all night, and it transforms into the light of day. I'm not sure if that's true, but that's the story."

"Well, how do we build the magic at night?" he asked.

Just then, a loud bell began to toll.

"You're about to find out, kid," said Phil the Gnome, "Now, we really do have to get going. You don't want to get caught out here when the darkness comes. Bad things happen in the darkness of the Yellow-Green Grasslands at night — bad, scary things. Even gnomes stay away from that kind of darkness. We get through that darkness together. And that's when the real fun starts."

"Where are we going?" asked Little Mark.

"Why, to the centre of it all," said Phil the Gnome, "Everyone gets together every night at the Town Centre Dance Party."

They arrived at the Town Centre at about the same time as

everyone else — just as the dark began to set in. They wouldn't have known it was the Town Centre in the day, because there wasn't really a town to be the centre of. There were no buildings or homes, just yellow-green grass like everywhere else. It wasn't the centre of anything at all. It was just where everybody was.

Little Mark was confused.

"A town ain't a bunch of buildings," said Phil the Gnome, "It's the people inside of them, and this particular town doesn't have any insides or outs, so the centre is where we all are. People come here every night to be together. The centre is where people meet."

As the light began to get darker, more creatures of all types began to arrive. The creatures were all shapes and sizes, and they were all laughing and dancing and making noise together that mixed itself into music. There were zebras dancing and clapping their hooves, birds fluttering around and chirping their songs. There were donkeys playing pattycake with tiny elephants, parrots flying about without their grey suits, singing songs that they made up themselves. Bears waltzed with bulls, cats with mice, and pirates jigged and played instruments from every story that Little Mark had ever had read to him in all his storytimes.

And there were gnomes. There were gnomes who played drums, gnomes who played guitars, gnomes who played pianos and tubas and xylophones. They blew horns, and jumped through hoops like circus performers and acrobats, summersaulting and tumbling through the yellow-green grass. Some were dressed like clowns, others like dancing Elvises, or hip-styled hipsters. Phil took his place upon a red rock tabletop, and began to spin records on a turntable, dancing and doing flips, or jumping up and clicking his heels as he spun his sounds. Little Mark stood behind him, looking down at the sea of motion with bright lights flashing, coloured spots, and strobes. They blinded Little Mark, but that didn't stop him from dancing along, listening to the music, and feeling its pure happiness and joy. The whole scene was chaos, but the kind of chaos that had an underlying flow, a rhythm, a beat.

As the night outside the Town Centre became pure darkness, two great pedestals grew from the earth at the feet of the dancers. On top were Bubbles and Stone, the giants they'd met at the wall when they first arrived. The platforms grew high above the crowd, and they beat giant bass drums, leading the dance and following along.

And then, quite suddenly, up from the centre of the crowd came a third platform.

"Weeblake!" yelled the crowd.

Little Mark marvelled at the familiar face that was so different from the man who he thought he had known so well. Seeing Weeblake above the crowd dancing in all his glory, he was reminded of the hours he had spent dancing with Freedrake. The two brothers danced with the same steps and movements, but the feeling was different. Weeblake looked natural. He wasn't trying to do anything other than dance.

Then, Weeblake stepped up to a microphone. Some people in the crowd stopped dancing to listen, shushing those around them into silence. Others began to play along in quiet tones, a background sound for Weeblake's speech.

"Beautiful people of all shapes and kind, wonderful creatures of this glorious night. Tonight, is a special night for no other reason than we are here, and we are together. We feel this moment together, in our breath, in our heartbeats, in the energy, the life, the joy, we share. We celebrate our freedom. Live free. Be free. You, are the magic. We, are the magic. We, be the magic. We, free the magic!"

The whole crowd let out a great cheer, and began to dance

even more ecstatically than before. Little Mark's newfound freedom was pure excitement. The dancing was contagious, and he danced a dance of pure joy and energy and grace. For hours they danced together, and made music, and laughed, and jumped. It was a night of rhythmic chaos, of fun that continued as they sang and danced the light into existence.

As the light descended and the music thumped on, Weeblake jumped from his pedestal and landed in the crowd, or rather on top of it. He was moved around, surfing on the hands of gnomes. They chanted his name, Weeblake's smile beaming, until he disappeared all at once with a flash. The pedestals of the giants shrank to the ground, and the giants walked amongst the crowd. Then, the music slowly became quieter, and then stopped altogether, replaced by a calm breeze that rustled through the yellow-green grass as everyone went on their way.

"Where's everyone going?" asked Little Mark, as Phil the Gnome made his turntables disappear.

"They're going off to have their day now," he said.

"They're going off to work?" asked Little Mark.

"Work?" Phil the Gnome chuckled, "No, kid. People don't work here. If they want to work, they go off to Malahat's land. Here they do what they want. Some run through the grass, others sleep, still more do their art, making stuff with their hands, paws, claws or hooves, depending on what they've got to make stuff with."

"Wow," said Little Mark, "I'd like to see some of that stuff."

"We can if you want," said Phil the Gnome.

"But I'm hungry," said Little Mark, "Let's eat first,"

"Then eat," said Phil the Gnome.

"But where can we go for breakfast?"

"We don't have to go anywhere," said Phil the Gnome, "Like I said, It's all right here."

"What's right here?"

"Food, energy, life – bend down and pick it up. The yellow-green grass is for more than just rabbits."

"You want me to eat grass?" said Little Mark, "Grass is alright for rabbits, but for little boys?"

"It's good for everybody," said Phil the Gnome, and he reached down and took a handful of grass and put it into his mouth, "It tastes like anything you want it to taste like."

Little Mark reached down and put some grass in his mouth. First it tasted like chocolate, and then like cotton candy, and then cookies and ice cream. Then Little Mark imagined a bigger meal, and soon it tasted like burgers, french fries, and pie. Pretty soon, they were both eating fistfuls of the yellow-green grass. They filled their bellies, and then they got sleepy.

"Let's pull up a patch of grass and get some sleep," said Phil the Gnome.

"Aren't you going to go back to your underground home with all the pizza boxes?" asked Little Mark.

"It's better here," said Phil the Gnome, "I ain't going back there."

They both pulled up a patch of grass, and went to sleep.

When they woke, Little Mark and Phil the Gnome were startled to find Weeblake standing above them. They both stood up at attention right away, as if they were caught doing something wrong.

"M-M-Mister Weeblake, sir, we weren't expecting you," said Phil the Gnome nervously. It wasn't like Phil to be nervous. He usually respected people less, the more he was supposed to, but it seemed Weeblake was the exception. He was bashful like a boy on the first day of school.

"Stop stammering," said Weeblake, "I'm just a man who knows some magic. I'm not the magic itself."

"Sorry, sir," said Phil the Gnome, "You just surprised me."

"Yes, well, that is what magic is, isn't it — surprise," said Weeblake pausing, "So, this is the special one from upstairs, is it? He looks normal to me."

"Yes, of course, because he is. That's what makes him so special," said Phil the Gnome.

Weeblake looked at Little Mark closely.

"So, you're the one who filled the houses and lit the lights in all my brother's lands?"

"I guess so," said Little Mark.

"I saw you dancing last night. You glow very brightly."

"That's what they say," said Little Mark, "I never see it myself. It's not something I try to do. It just happens."

"Well, happening is quite a talent," said Weeblake, "Happening might be the most important talent of them all. My brother has a keen eye for talent. How is my brother?"

"I don't think I really know," said Little Mark, "All the time that I spent with him I think he was acting. I think he was being who he thought I wanted him to be. I don't know if I really know him at all."

"Exactly," said Weeblake, "My brother isn't ever who he is. That's how he gets what he wants."

"With Phil the Gnome's help, I got out of there," he said.

"Yes, we like Phil around here," said Weeblake, "And we like you too. I do hope that you stay for a while, and I hope you have fun. That is what we do here – we stay, and we have fun."

"I should probably be getting home sometime," said Little Mark, "But I suppose I should stay here for a while, and try to have some fun."

"You shouldn't always do the things you should," said

Weeblake, "And fun isn't something you try to do. It's something that happens."

"Well, then I guess I will stay and happen for a while," said Little Mark.

Then, Weeblake smiled a wild smile, clapped his hands, and disappeared in a flash.

Chapter Thirteen

A Giant Eats Himself

Each evening unfolded in a similar way. As the inky darkness descended on the Yellow-Green Grasslands, the creatures would all join together in the Town Centre to ride out the darkness and the music would begin to make itself. It was spontaneous. Everyone just listened to each other, swapping sounds and instruments, blending naturally into song. They danced, they sang, they played, and after a while the giants, Bubbles and Stone, would rise up on their pedestals and guide the beat. Then, Weeblake would rise from the crowd to spin and dance and sing poetry. Phil spun his records, and everyone played and danced and sang along. Little Mark danced along too, glowing and glowing and glowing. As the light came up again each morning, Weeblake would dive off his pedestal and into the crowd, surfing for a while and then disappearing dramatically with a flourish. Then the music would still, and everyone would have their day in the light. Each day was exactly the same as the last, and yet completely different, much the way that all days in any world tend to be.

Little Mark and Phil the Gnome usually stuck to their

routine. They started the morning with a big meal of yellow-green grass that changed flavour depending on what they wanted to eat. The yellow-green grass never introduced a new taste. It only became what they had already experienced. Little Mark didn't mind, because he only ate what he liked anyway. So, he ate cookies and chips everyday, which were just as healthy as everything else, because it was all made of the yellow-green grass.

Then they went to sleep. It was unclear exactly how long any day or night or sleep was, except that it was exactly as long as it was supposed to be and not any longer. When they woke, they would be surrounded by bunnies who were always munching away on the yellow-green grass. The rabbits would join them as they wandered through the Yellow-Green Grasslands, finding the fields of artists hard at work. The busiest were the gnomes with easels full of canvases that they painted with the brightest, most vivid colours. The paintings were so joyful, and when they were finished, they would all sit together and watch them dry. But, as they dried, a strange thing happened — the images faded into blankness. This made Little Mark sad at first — such beautiful things lost so quickly, but the gnome explained that it wasn't the picture they wanted, but the painting, so the gnomes could paint their pictures again and again and again. Other creatures sculpted statues that kept their shape in the light, but melted into nothing in the night. This left them something to sculpt the next day. They had whole fields of sand in which they drew words and pictures and poetry that would blow away in the winds, and they would create castles that would crumble to dust to be built again. They were always creating fresh new visions that would come to life before their eyes, and then disappear, leaving them something again to create.

Then they would hear the bell toll and would find their

way to the Town Centre to come together to survive the Yellow-Green Grasslands at night.

And each night, they would dance together to bring in the light.

The days and nights blended together, a cascading series of moments drifting into the next, full of highlights that they played back to each other in the quieter times.

Dance at night, sleep in mornings, and partake in the art of the afternoons.

Each day, they would see what was on the easel of each artist, what figure was being created, what story was being told to all who took the time to look.

And then they would dance.

One day, while they were looking at some sculptures, they saw a group of creatures on a hill in the distance where nobody usually went. They decided to take a look to see what was going on. When they arrived, they saw some of the creatures crowded into a circle with worried looks on their faces. In the centre of the circle was the biggest of all the creatures – Stone the Giant, who beat the bass drum every night on his pedestal. Now he was sitting in the middle of a crowd, and had one of his giant bare feet in his mouth, all the way up to his ankle. Little Mark looked at Phil the Gnome astonished to see such a thing.

"Is this some sort of performance art?" asked Little Mark.

"This ain't art, kid," he said, "It's life. This is how it works. It's gonna be one of those days that you remember."

The whole crowd was silent, watching as Stone the Giant began to eat himself. It happened slowly, but no one had any intention to stop him. It was not long before he had his other foot in his mouth up to its ankle too. He ate up to his ankles and then to his knees, slowly, silently, methodically. He swallowed to his knees, and then he ate up to his thighs and waist, his mouth getting bigger and stretching more and more to accommodate his giant waist and torso. He contorted himself slowly, eating, swallowing, and digesting himself. Whole hours seemed to take forever, and yet no time at all. All the watchers in the gathering crowd watched on silently, with worried looks on their faces. There was sadness, and tears flowed in some. When the lips of his mouth reached his belly button, they curled around himself, and he sucked in his final bite, and then the whole ground began to shake.

"Hold on kid," yelled Phil the Gnome, as the rumbling intensified, "This affects everything."

The shaking became so intense that they fell to the ground. They shook and shook, and they rumbled and rumbled, until what was left of Stone the Giant became a ball, and began to roll. The whole land tilted in one direction, and all the crowd tried to hang on. Those in his way parted so they wouldn't get crushed by Stone the Giant as his rolling took on momentum. Everyone else just held on so as not to roll away with Stone. The world remained tilted for a time, and everyone just held on until eventually, it became even again.

Then they all dusted themselves off and stood up straight.

The bell tolled, and the people moved to the Town Centre.

Chapter Fourteen

A New Giant is Born

When they arrived at the Town Centre, the evening started much the same way as it would ordinarily. The music spontaneously created itself out of the players. Their sound matched the melancholic mood of those who had witnessed Stone the Giant eating himself. The sound grew and, as usual, a pedestal rose from the earth, and upon it, was Bubbles the Giant. Bubbles danced alone and beat his drum like a heartbeat for his departed partner. Over and over, he beat the drum, until Weeblake's pedestal rose up from the crowd, and everyone hushed for him to speak.

"Today we witnessed the end of Stone the Giant, the beat of our time. The sounds we made together will echo in our memory and in the songs we will sing in the times to come. We remember him for who he was and what we did together. Tonight, we celebrate a life, and all life. Tonight, we dance for Stone."

The mood of the music changed as the players began to see all the different parts of the life of Stone, and not simply that he was gone. After a time, sadness turned to appreciation, the music took on a joy of remembrance, of Stone as he was, in the crowd, on his pedestal, a centre of the Town Centre. It became a celebration not of the giant that was gone, but the giant who had been.

Suddenly, another pedestal began to rise up from the crowd, up to the highest spot. On top of that pedestal was a single gnome – a small, young gnome in a clown suit, who Little Mark had seen Phil the Gnome talking to at times before. Phil seemed surprised that she was the one to go on top. When the pedestal reached its peak, it stopped growing, but the gnome on top had just begun. Now, the gnome herself, began to grow. She grew quickly, so quickly that she burst out of her clown costume, her hair falling from her head, as she began to take the form of the creature she was to be. The gnome became a giant before their eyes. She danced around and cheered in her new body. The tears of loss for Stone, turned to joy and celebration for the new giant.

"My friends, you honour the memory of Stone," said Weeblake, "You honour what he was and what you were together. But now, we begin a new era, a new beat, a new part of your life, and that of the world. This is life renewed. This is life regenerated. The new giant is upon the pedestal! Welcome the new Giant: Earth! Now is the era of the Giant Earth!"

With that, the giant who had so recently been a gnome dressed as a clown, began to bang upon her drum in a different beat than they had been beating before. She beat out a solo and then everyone joined in to play along and a new song was born. All those who danced felt the energy come alive again as the music reached a higher level, a dance of hope and remembrance. They all danced through the night until the light descended at the end of the song.

*\ *\ *

The next morning, while eating a breakfast of yellow-green grass, Little Mark felt uneasy.

"Why did Stone the Giant do that to himself?" he asked.

"He was a giant, kid," said Phil the Gnome, "That's what they do."

"But why?"

"It was his time, I guess," he said, "The giants are the signs of the times and maybe his time was up. The giants tell us who we are at a time in history. Everyone knows who they are because of who the giants are — a new giant means it's a new era."

"But how did he know it was his time?"

"That I don't know," said Phil the Gnome, "Maybe there's like a button in his brain that gets pressed, or maybe he's got a plan. All the giants know they gotta go sometime. It's part of the deal with being a giant. We know it, they know it. It's understood."

"Does that mean that Bubbles is next?"

"It doesn't mean that at all, kid," he said, "There ain't no rules that way. It could be Bubbles, or it could be Earth, it could be tomorrow, or it could be in a thousand years. Each time it's different. But the one thing you can count on, is that they will be there, and they will be gone. That's life."

"And then a gnome turns into a giant to replace them?" asked Little Mark.

"That's about the extent of it, kid."

"And it could be any gnome?"

"Yep."

"Even you?"

"Even me."

"How do they choose?"

"We don't choose – it just happens," said Phil the Gnome, "We don't know why. We just know it does."

"And where did Stone the Giant go?"

"That's the big question isn't it. We all wonder, but none of us really know. That's the difference between here and over in his brother's land. They've got an answer for everything and they're sure about it, until they're not, and then they're sure of something else. Here we don't know, but we accept it. Sometimes we make up stories to make us feel better, but that's all they are — stories. Truth is, it's a mystery, maybe the biggest one of them all. That makes some people nervous, but I like it that way. If we knew everything, then we wouldn't be surprised, and we would never change."

Little Mark felt uneasy. He wasn't sure he liked surprises.

Chapter Fifteen

Faeries are Real

The days and nights continued as they had before and yet were completely different. Maybe it was the different sound of the music or the style of the ceremony, maybe it was the people themselves who had changed because of what they had seen. Regardless, it really was a new era in the Yellow-Green Grasslands. While it was technically the era of the giants Bubbles and Earth, the biggest change in the festivities was the little glowing boy who was twice the size of a gnome — the one who danced with such intensity. Little Mark became so popular at the Town Centre dance parties that some creatures liked him even more than Weeblake himself, but Little Mark didn't seem to notice.

Each morning Little Mark and Phil the Gnome munched away at their morning meal of yellow-green grass and Little Mark would ask questions about everything in the underground. It all seemed to run without rules and no direction. He wondered about Weeblake, who, true to his magic, would keep himself secret and surprise people, showing up when they least expected. Weeblake said he was one of his own subjects just like everyone else, and he followed the same rules, which amounted to almost none. Little Mark wondered where this was all going.

"So, this is it?" asked Little Mark to Phil the Gnome, one morning after a particularly long night of dancing.

"This is what?" asked Phil the Gnome.

"This is everything? There's here and there's there and there's nothing more than that? It's just Freedrake's or Weeblake's and that's all?"

"As far as I can see, that's right. There are legends, but I don't know if those are true."

"Legends?"

"Yeah," said Phil the Gnome, "People talk about a land, a place that is here but isn't. They say it exists but doesn't. Maybe that's where the magic comes from. Maybe that's where Stone the Giant went. Maybe that's where the faeries come from, but I've never seen one of them, so who knows if they're real."

"Faeries?"

"Yep faeries. Some people say we got faeries down here. They say they can fly around wherever they want, but they sure don't fly around here."

"Well, why don't they come here?"

"Maybe they don't exist. Maybe this is just it. Or maybe they're too classy for this place. What would they want with a bunch of sweaty gnomes and vagabonds who dance all night? Some say they watch from a distance, flying so fast that we can't even see them. I don't know. That's what legends are – things that people want to believe that might or might not be true."

Little Mark felt sad. If this was the whole world down here, what was he doing? What was his purpose? His whole reason for coming down here was to explore, and he wasn't going anywhere or doing anything. This was supposed to be the land of imagination, so why couldn't he imagine what to do or where to go? He began to feel glum. Maybe it was time to find his way back home.

That night they danced as usual, forgetting for a moment those difficult questions. As the night hit its height, a gnome Little Mark hadn't seen before, tapped him on the shoulder and beckoned him to follow. He followed to the edge of the Town Centre, into the deep grass.

"I've watched you dance," said the gnome, "I like how you glow."

"Thanks," said Little Mark.

"This isn't it," he whispered, "This isn't everything. There is another place down here."

"Really?"

"Yes. There is a place that you cannot even imagine."

"What is it? Where?"

The gnome smiled in a way that Little Mark had never seen a gnome smile before.

"Doing this is against the rules," said the gnome, becoming even more mysterious.

Then Little Mark got the surprise of his life. First, the gnome pulled off his hat and then his beard. Underneath, he had a smooth face and long, straight black hair. This gnome was no gnome at all. The green suit dropped to the grass, revealing a silky dress of sparkle that seemed to be made of light itself. She had two big, brown eyes, and soft, bronze skin that looked like light as well. And she had two sparkling wings that were resting at her back, ready to fly.

"Are you a faerie?" asked a dumfounded Little Mark.

"What do you think?" asked the faerie.

"You don't look like the faeries in the books."

"I'm not supposed to look like a book. I'm supposed to look like I do," said the faerie, "The people who tell you what I should look like, have never actually seen me before. What do you think?"

"I've never seen anything look more like a faerie than you do," said Little Mark decidedly, "What are you doing here?"

"Why wouldn't I be?" said the faerie, "I love the music, and I've been dancing with you since you got here."

"But I never saw you. Why didn't you talk to me?"

"I didn't want to interrupt you," she said, "You looked so happy."

"I am happy but I need to see something new. How can I get to your world?" asked Little Mark.

"Why do you want to go to my world?" asked the faerie.

"I guess I'm a looker," said Little Mark, "I look for things. I don't know how to live without looking."

"Well, then, if you'd like to come to my land, you'll have to learn how to fly," said the faerie.

"How do I do that?"

"You already know how."

Then she gave an astonished Little Mark a kiss on his cheek, and then leapt gracefully into the air. Her wings fluttered effortlessly and caught the air, lifting her up into the sky. She buzzed overtop the dancers who all stopped and pointed at her before she was gone.

"Who are you?" whispered Little Mark into the Yellow-Green Grasslands as he stood alone at the edge of the darkness.

Chapter Sixteen

How to get to the Land Beyond Imagination

Nobody knew why it was that the rabbits stopped dancing. Maybe they stopped being afraid of the dark and didn't need to come into the Town Centre every night. Maybe they just wanted to eat grass all day and all night, imagining it tasted like carrots or maybe it tasted like itself, and they enjoyed it so much that they didn't need to be with the others making music and dancing. Everyone agreed that it was impossible to understand the minds of rabbits, and rabbits would do exactly what rabbits would do and nothing other. Regardless, they stopped dancing, and they got fat, and the fatter they got, the less they wanted to dance, until no one knew what to do about the whole situation because there really wasn't anything to be done if it wasn't the rabbits doing it themselves. Still, as everyone went about their days, they couldn't stop thinking about the rabbits.

Little Mark, too, couldn't focus on the nights. He liked them fine when he was dancing, but he lost the anticipation that had filled his day when he had first arrived. He couldn't stop thinking about his visit from the faerie, about her kiss, about the Land Beyond Imagination.

And he wondered about how to fly.

He could fly? Really?

He found that hard to believe, but then he had never thought that he could glow before, and now that was happening regularly. He asked Weeblake about it when he appeared one morning while he and Phil the Gnome were walking through the Yellow-Green Grasslands.

"Lots of people can fly who don't think they can. We all do it differently. You just have to find your own way," said Weeblake, "Why do you want to fly anyway?"

"Well, the faerie said that I have to fly in order to get to the Land Beyond Imagination."

"You want to start meeting with the faeries, do you?" said Weeblake. "Not everyone is allowed into their world, and many who have been there, didn't even know it. More still, are there right now, but can't see it either. It's as much about how you look as where. It is a place that can't be seen until it is believed, but can't be believed unless it is seen. Flying helps with that — however you do it."

"But how do I do it?" asked Little Mark.

"I'll show you my favourite way to fly, but yours will most certainly be different."

Weeblake clapped his hands, and the ground below him raised him up on the pedestal, just like at the dance parties, but this time it kept going higher. He rose until he was almost out of sight and then the pedestal disappeared and Weeblake came hurtling down towards them.

"He's not flying, he's falling," yelled Little Mark, jumping out of the way.

"If you want to fly, you have to find your own way," yelled Weeblake smiling, as he sped toward them. Inches away, he clapped his hands and disappeared an instant before he hit the ground.

"I'm trying to be serious and all he does is try to scare me and joke around," said Little Mark to Phil the Gnome with frustration, as he stood up and dusted himself off, "The faerie said I could fly, but how am I supposed to do that?"

"Don't ask me," said Phil the Gnome, "I'm a digger. Diggers don't fly. The best advice I ever gave or got, was to follow my feet."

And that's what Little Mark did that night. Everyone was dancing and playing and singing and making music, forgetting, for the moment, the missing bunnies eating yellow-green grass alone in the dark fields. Little Mark was dancing too, but his heart wasn't in it, his head wasn't in it. He was thinking about flying and about imagining the Land Beyond Imagination. It didn't make a whole lot of sense to leave, but he felt like it was the right thing to do. He waved to Weeblake on his pedestal and smiled at Phil the Gnome who was spinning his records and dancing. The next thing he knew, he was walking through the dancers and musicians and past the fattened rabbits who hopped slowly along with him for a while, as he did what he was told never to do.

He walked alone into the darkness of the Yellow-Green Grasslands at night.

Chapter Seventeen

The Cemetery of Ex-Pets

Little Mark had never been afraid of the dark. In fact, he liked the dark. Sometimes he liked it even more than the light. His brothers and sisters would go to bed with their night lights on, but he liked to stay awake and just stare into the darkness trying to see what might be there. The darkness of the Yellow-Green Grasslands, even though it was the darkest darkness that had ever been, was not particularly dark for Little Mark because this journey into the unknown made him glow even brighter than usual.

But the darkness of the Yellow-Green Grasslands was no ordinary darkness. It was magically made to make even the bravest afraid. If the yellow-green grass could taste like whatever food you wanted, the darkness of the Yellow-Green Grasslands at night would find whatever fear was in your heart and make it real. That is why everyone went into the Town Centre at night. Dancing together, their fears were forgotten. But Little Mark was on this journey alone, and even though he glowed, the darkness still held its magic. It wasn't long before he was faced by his fears.

Little Mark was young and did not yet know what he should be afraid of, but then, most people are not afraid of what they should be, because fear is not logical. Fear is a feeling that comes from something small that gets bigger. The more that we think about it, the bigger it becomes — much bigger than the thing that we were afraid of in the first place. In Little Mark's case, he never knew what he was afraid of, until the darkness of the Yellow-Green Grasslands introduced him to the Cemetery of Ex-Pets. When he saw that, his heart jumped into his throat. He was faced with a fear he had never known before, made real, right before his eyes. He knew immediately that this was a fear that he couldn't run away from.

In the haunting blackness of the darkest night, Little Mark came upon row on row of the stone-grey tombstones of all the world's past pets. Floating above each of the tombstones were the pets themselves. They were pale, ghostly, translucent versions of themselves, that hovered in the air with leering faces. Most had died before Little Mark was born, but he recognized some of them from the stories that his brothers and sisters told, and from family photos that had become part of his own memory. Others were completely anonymous cats or birds, lizards or fish, that Little Mark had no knowledge of at all. The one pet he did recognize was Arthur, the little, black, curly-haired dog, who had been his dog until he had died just a few months before. Little Mark remembered the funeral. Arthur got hit by a car and had to be put to sleep to ease his pain. Now, Arthur's ghost was right here, in front of him.

"Hello Mark," said Arthur the Ex-Pet, "You are lucky to find me. This cemetery is a dangerous place for some people."

"Uh, yes," said Little Mark, "But I don't feel lucky right now."

"Why not?" asked Arthur the Ex-Pet.

"I'm not sure," said Little Mark, "Maybe it's because I'm surrounded by the ghosts of dead animals who can talk."

"It's funny," said Arthur the Ex-Pet, "I am surrounded by them too, but I don't have your attitude. It's that attitude that makes us ghosts act the way we do. If everyone acted like that to you, what kind of attitude do you think you would have?"

"I'm sorry," said Little Mark, "But I'm not used to seeing ghosts, and I didn't know you could talk."

"Well, we're not used to seeing little boys anymore either, not live ones anyways," said Arthur the Ex-Pet, "Remember, this is our cemetery. We didn't ask you to come. We don't come into your living room anymore, but now you've come into ours."

"I'm sorry," said Little Mark.

"Of course you are," said Arthur the Ex-Pet, "Now tell me. What brings you to our lovely cemetery? Did someone die, or are you going to die to get in?"

"No," said Little Mark, "I just walked out into the darkness and found you here."

"Where are you going?" asked Arthur the Ex-Pet.

"Well," said Little Mark, "I'm trying to get to the Land Beyond Imagination where all the faeries live."

"Do your parents know where you are?" asked Arthur the Ex-Pet.

"No, they don't," said Little Mark, "They probably don't even know I'm gone, but unless I learn to fly and get to the Land Beyond Imagination, I can't imagine ever going home."

"Well, you are lucky again," said Arthur the Ex-Pet, "You can go through the Cemetery of Ex-Pets to get there, and I know just the person to get you there."

"Who?" asked Little Mark.

"Me!" said Arthur the Ex-Pet, "Wanna go walkies?"

That's what Little Mark used to say to him not too long before.

"Stay close," he continued, "The bite of these dogs is worse than their bark."

Little Mark followed closely behind Arthur the Ex-Pet, who wound his way through the tombstones. The ghosts of the ex-pets howled and screamed, and Little Mark became afraid, so he focused on Arthur's curly, little, wagging tail. They passed countless tombstones and their ghostly guardians – cats and rats and dogs and hamsters and goldfish and monkeys and mongooses and many, many more – and the more they passed, the more they saw off into the horizon.

"So many tombstones," said Little Mark, "I never knew my family had so many pets."

"The pets were never yours," said Arthur the Ex-Pet, "We are all ourselves, and together we are us. Down every line, every family, every being, is related to every other one somewhere. We're all part of the same family so that means that all the pets are related too. All the pets from all the families and all their cemeteries, all end up here. This isn't your or my Cemetery of Ex-Pets — it is everyone's."

"But why did I have to come here in order to get to the Land Beyond Imagination?" asked Little Mark.

"You didn't." said Arthur the Ex-Pet, "But you did, and you can, so unless you have a better plan, I suggest you follow me."

"But the faerie I met said that I needed to fly to get there."

"Oh, you think you need to fly, do you? We can do that too. I know two ways, but which one we choose will depend on you," said Arthur the Ex-Pet.

"What do you mean?" asked Little Mark.

"You know me, Mark," said Arthur the Ex-Pet, "I was there when you were born. I was there when you took your first steps. I have always been a good boy. I can take you there if you trust me, or I can make you into something that can get there itself."

"What do you mean?" asked Little Mark again.

Then, Arthur the Ex-Pet grew and grew, making Little Mark littler and littler before the big dog's form. His face was leering and howling like all the other ex-pets. His big, giant teeth opened wide, making him scary and menacing, right before Little Mark's eyes.

"I mean," said Arthur the Ex-Pet, "Ghosts can get there quite easily. I can turn you into my kind, if you like. You can be a ghost and float wherever you will. You can fly, but first, you must die!"

Little Mark became terrified of Arthur. His heart thumped deeply against the inside of his chest. This was it. His childhood pet who had died was now going to kill him, and there was nothing he could do about it. He remembered Arthur's death, how much he had cried. He had always wondered where Arthur had gone when he died, and now he was here. How did he get to this place? How had Arthur become this? This was not the Arthur he knew, the Arthur he remembered.

"What happened to you, Arthur?" asked Little Mark, "You weren't a scary dog. You weren't even my dog. You were my friend. We played together. More than even my brothers and sisters, we were friends."

With that, Arthur shrank down again to his regular size. He began wagging his curly little tail, and started to lick Little Mark's face. He became the Arthur that Little Mark knew once again.

"So, you chose the first way," said Arthur the Ex-Pet, "Good. Ghosts are just like they were when they were alive. It's how you see them that changes. If you'd seen me with fear, you'd have changed me into something that could have turned you into a ghost. But you knew who I was. You remembered me. We were friends. I'll take you there. We'll fly together."

With that, he jumped into Little Mark's arms, and they leapt together, into the air.

"Hold on," yelled Arthur the Ex-Pet, and Little Mark held tight to the little black dog, with the curly black tail, and began to float up into the sky.

* * *

A pale dawn was stirring as Little Mark held on to Arthur the Ex-Pet, flying with his friend above all the ghostly spirits of ex-pets and the cavernous lands. He looked down at the factories and roads of Freedrake's lands, and saw his subjects working away like ants to build more of everything. Next to that, were the Yellow-Green Grasslands, and Weeblake's subjects, settling to sleep after a night of giants and pedestals and dancing. The wall between the lands, so tall from below, seemed tiny from the sky. In the morning twilight, the dark and light were joining together.

"I'm not really sure where we're going," said Arthur the Ex-Pet, "We ghosts are more floaters than flyers, and I've never been this high before. We've got to hurry because I fade into nothing when the light comes up completely, and then you won't be able to hold onto me any longer."

They neared the cavern's roof, looking up at the roots of plants coming out of the top of the cave. Then they saw a crack in the roof opening up. A bright, white light began shining through the crack, blinding them as they looked up.

Arthur floated them towards it, but as they neared, from out of nowhere, came Freedrake Malahat, zooming along on a motorized flightbike, as Bill the Bug buzzed behind.

"Come back," yelled Freedrake, the old man's lab coat flapping as he soared through the underground sky, "We need you."

"Stay away from him," yelled another voice from the other direction. It was Weeblake. He was riding a magic energy surfboard with Phil the Gnome surfing along on the tip of the board, "We need you, Little Mark. We miss you."

"This is my favourite way to fly," said Phil the Gnome to Little Mark with a wink.

The two brothers grabbed at Little Mark, jostling each other and trying to take him for their own. Little Mark hung on to Arthur the Ex-Pet, but they yanked and pulled like little boys fighting over a toy, so enwrapped in their squabble that they did not notice that they had knocked Arthur the Ex-Pet out of Little Mark's hands.

Both Little Mark and Arthur the Ex-Pet began to tumble down towards the ground. Little Mark felt real fear as he fell, picking up speed as the ground came closer.

Then, all of the sudden there was a flash, and everything stopped. Little Mark just paused and floated, and Arthur the Ex-Pet didn't disappear in the light, but hung, suspended in the air, looking up as a figure began to emerge from the crack in the sky. This was their first glimpse of the Garden Queen.

The twins stopped fighting and stared up above.

"My gracious, my children. Will you ever change? Can you not see that the boy is meant for neither of your worlds, that the world that you have created is not for any child, but for your own selfish selves? The only children you are making it for is you, and you are the oldest children of all. And now, as you are acting like children, you must be treated like children."

With that, she reached down and grabbed Freedrake and Weeblake, each by the scruff of their necks, like a momma cat carrying her baby kittens.

"Stop it Mother," they both cried like little children.

Bill and Phil and Little Mark and Arthur the Ex-Pet hovered for a time, until a group of faeries descended and took them in their arms, up through the crack in the underground sky, and into the light of the Land Beyond Imagination.

Chapter Eighteen

The Secret Garden

"I still don't know how to fly," said Little Mark, to the faerie who was carrying him upwards. She was the same faerie he had met at the dance. He felt embarrassed because he couldn't fly on his own.

"Flying is just like swimming through the air in any way that you can," she said, "That's what we're doing now, right? You don't need wings to fly. That's what friends are for. Wings are for sharing. You can just enjoy the ride."

Little Mark was astonished by the Garden Queen's Garden. He was floating through unimaginable beauty in the arms of a real-life faerie. He could never have imagined a heaven like this. Everything here was clearer, brighter, more perfect than a picture, like he could feel the heartbeat in things. It was like seeing the sun for the very first time.

Everywhere he looked, the plants were in bloom. There were trees laden with fruit, branches heavy with flowers, plants of all sizes and shapes, leaves of every shade, and bright, vivid, clear, colours. There was a calm bustle of hummingbirds and bees, and butterflies flittering from flower to flower, ladybugs swimming backwards through the air, and fountains and streams and mountains and sunshine. It was a natural, harmonious peace, with a humming calm that was quieter than silence. The faeries dropped them off on the grass at the base of a large tree, and the Garden Queen was still scolding her boys who she dropped in a heap.

"Ow, ouch," they complained, "Let go, Mum, let go!"

They all couldn't help but laugh at the sight of two old men being scolded by their mother.

"My goodness, my children," said the Garden Queen, "You have made a mess of things for far too long. When are you going to grow up?"

"It's his fault," they both yelled.

"You kids," said the Garden Queen, "You are so busy talking that you have forgotten to listen. You just separate yourselves and point your fingers over your fences. Your fences make you both smaller. You are so busy being right that you can't see when you're wrong. Don't you know what good you could do if only you worked together?"

Freedrake and Weeblake continued, wild with their accusations, each blaming the other, explaining to everyone how they could never, ever be together.

"If you must," said the Garden Queen finally losing patience, "Walk away for a time, but you must know that you have common purpose. Come back again with a plan to work together for everyone and everything. You must live with your brother together. No more fences."

Furious, they each stomped off in opposite directions.

Little Mark stood before the tall Garden Queen who turned her attention to her new guests. Phil the Gnome and Bill the Bug wanted to follow Weeblake and Freedrake, but she stopped them.

"My children need some time alone," said the Garden

Queen, "They must understand the mess they are making. You two shall join us."

Little Mark was hypnotized by the Garden Queen. Royal in her resplendent gown and crown of flowers, she was the statue from his auntie's garden come to life. Her voice, like a song, had poise and power and grace.

"I'm sorry for my boys and all they've done," said the Garden Queen, "They used to be such good kids until they grew up. Then they became the biggest children imaginable. Now they're too big for themselves and everyone else. It might be time to put them into their place if they can't find it themselves."

The treehouse palace she called the Pavilion, was not a house in the trees, nor made from trees at all, but of them. It was a living house, that grew into its shape, not dead wood for walls, but a living tree that was molded into elaborate and beautiful rooms. There were flowers on every table, live ones that grew out of the tables and walls themselves. There were rooms in the trunk, rooms in the branches, rooms in the roots and the leaves. Everything was growing inside and out, such that there was no inside or out, but rather both together.

"All the worlds are of the garden," said the Garden Queen, "It is the originator of all things. All that grows, from above and below, comes from here. All the seasons come to life in a continuous cycle from the garden and into the world."

The garden extended out from the Pavilion, but most of the land was left to grow wild. As they walked into the wilds, the Garden Queen picked from the plants and they ate all manner of berry and pear and plum and leaf, each with a taste of impossible deliciousness. She led them around, as they ran through the forests and climbed through the trees, enjoying the wild nature. Sometimes she would just touch something, and blossoms and flowers would burst forth, and she would just smile as they all stared on in a dream.

Arthur the Ex-Pet sniffed at all the trees and plants, and Bill the Bug was amazed by all the insects there who flitted whichever way they wished. Even Phil the Gnome was mesmerized by the faeries.

The faeries giggled and poked their heads up over hedges at first, getting a closer look at the strangers, chatting amongst themselves. As they got used to the strangers, the faeries became less shy, and fluttered about like butterflies. Little Mark spied the faerie he knew, who was watching him play from behind a tree. Then, as he was talking to the Queen, she appeared, right beside him.

"Little Mark, have you met Ai?" asked the Garden Queen, "She's a very special faerie."

Just then a hummingbird flew up and whispered something into the Garden Queen's ear.

"I'm sorry but it seems I must go and check up on my children," she said, "Ai could you please give these gentlemen the rest of the tour and make them at home?"

With a bow and a wave, she was flying away.

Ai took them to an orchard of apples where they all tasted the sour-sweet fruit together. Phil munched loudly and Bill bore his big nose into the fruit and sucked out all the flavour. Arthur was content to walk next to Little Mark with a skip in his step. Little Mark's shyness dissolved into all the questions he wanted to ask the faerie.

"What, where, why is this place?" he asked all at once.

"This is the Secret Garden," said Ai, "We are all the worlds at once. We cultivate and sew, nurture and grow, all that is alive in the world. The seasons happen together — winter, spring, summer, and fall — all at the same time, getting ready for where they must go."

Little Mark was astonished. Now, he was finally learning the truth.

"And what about Freedrake and Weeblake. Are they really the Garden Queen's children?"

"We are all her children, I supposed," said Ai, "But the boys are her first. They got along when they were children but they have become so different. They are so competitive. They can't stand to lose to the other at anything and fight over everything. They fight so much that they have forgotten about the rest of the world and all the people in it."

"But why do they care about me?" asked Little Mark, "I'm just a little boy."

"I don't know if they really care about you, except to compete with each other," said Ai, "If you choose them, then they think they are right. And they also get the show – your show. You're the one who makes people watch. If you're with them, then everyone is with them."

When Ai mentioned the show, Bill the Bug and Phil the Gnome became uncomfortable. They could not deny it any longer. They admitted it. They hadn't been telling Little Mark the truth. They had been tricking their friend. The cameras were on the whole time. He was the biggest show everywhere.

"We're sorry, kid," said Phil the Gnome, "I always believed everything I ever told you, even if it wasn't everything I could have told you. I was looking out for you. It could have gone a lot worse."

"I'm sorry for lying to you all the time," said Bill the Bug, "My cameras might be neutral, but where I point them isn't. It doesn't mean that I don't care about you. I was hoping for the best for everyone, and not just you. But you're the greatest — you dance to dance and not to sell the glow."

Little Mark was quiet for a while. How could he trust his

friends again? Sure, they had done amazing things together, but how could he rely on them to tell him the truth.

"I want to forgive you, but your lies hurt me," said Little Mark after a while, "Worse than that, they hurt everybody. You tried to make lying okay. Everyone loses when you lie, and no one can trust you again. I can't trust you again. But I have also learned so much from you. I have done things with you that I will always remember, and you are always going to be a part of all of them. If you are really sorry, I can forgive you. I can still love you, but I can't trust you."

Bill the Bug and Phil the Gnome apologized again for letting him down, and it made them sad whenever they thought of it. They all tried to forget the lies so that they could still see the Secret Garden clearly. Ai showed them through the seasons, flying along and telling stories about all the things growing. Arthur followed along as well, still firmly at Little Mark's side — he felt comforted that Arthur was there and would be forever.

They looked at plants from all the seasons, but did not venture too far into the wilds in case they got lost. They were in the summer surrounded by palm trees, when a hummingbird buzzed up, and whispered something into Ai's ear.

"We must return to the Pavilion quickly," said Ai, "Those silly boys can't work it out. They think that some stupid contest is going to solve everything. They think they win if the other loses. They are going to have a race, and they want to start right away."

Chapter Nineteen

A Race around the Seasons

Freedrake and Weeblake both greeted Little Mark coldly when he went to talk to them before the race. They were hurt that Little Mark hadn't chosen them. They just ignored him as they readied themselves for the race — Weeblake waxing up his magic energy surfboard – a surfboard that rode on the life force of magic, and Malahat was tweaking the engine of his mechanical flightbike. The race was around the corner of each of the seasons and then back home to the Pavilion. It would take them around the vast expanse of the Secret Garden, through the wildest parts that no one ever visited. The Pavilion was the centre of the garden, where all of the seasons met in the kind of weather that was comfortable for everyone, so they used it as the start and finish line. The start of the race would be easy, but as they got farther away from the centre, the racers would have to deal with the difficult weather and wildness of each of all the seasons.

"Why are you guys doing this?" asked Little Mark to the brothers.

"To prove who's right," said Freedrake, "The winner of the race promises to live by the other one's rules."

"Why would you do that?" asked Little Mark.

"Because whoever can build a better system should lead the world," said Weeblake, "He thinks his flightbike is better than my board. He thinks machines are better than magic. If that's right, then he should lead. Otherwise, it's me."

"A contest is the only way to solve it," said Freedrake, "Otherwise, we'll just keep fighting forever."

"What about co-operation and working together?" asked Little Mark.

They shushed him and told him to keep his opinions to himself.

The faeries greeted the race with quiet concern. They were interested in the outcome, but they worried about the garden. This was a place for everything, so all of the ideas in the world should be welcome here too. If one set of ideas won, it didn't make all the other ideas wrong. This competition wasn't helping anyone. There was room in the garden for everyone if they worked together. They didn't like the idea of the race at all.

"The race begins and ends in spring," said the Garden Queen, "From here, you proceed to the pole of spring, and then around the poles of summer, autumn and winter, and then spring again, before returning here to the Pavilion — exactly where you started."

Freedrake revved up his scooter and Weeblake primed his board, each readying himself for the start. Ai hovered above them and then dropped a single rose. As soon as it hit the ground, the brothers were off.

It was a race of science and magic. While the possibilities of both might be limitless, each needed energy to use. Freedrake's flightbike had the ability to convert light into movement, so the sunshine of the spring had him cruising high over the bursting buds and flowers. Weeblake's board flew, not by some special engine, but because of the magic of the rider himself. Magic is everywhere and only limited by a person's ability to make it real. Weeblake could focus the energy of the magic to speed his board through the sky effortlessly. The excitement of the race, and the spring sun had his energy flying high, just like his board. The twin old men sped through the warm sun, their white hair flowing behind.

But this was a very long race.

The brothers teased and taunted, threw spells and played tricks on each other as they flew. They didn't want to hurt each other, but if they could knock each other off course, they could gain an advantage. Early in the race, Weeblake shot a few energy balls that Freedrake deflected, and Freedrake shot some electrical charges that Weeblake blocked. Each attack was useless against the other's defences, but the errant attacks landed in the garden, destroying whole rows of roses and wild daisies and trees. The faeries followed behind, working desperately to put out all the fires, saving whole species of plants and trees. As the brothers flew, the Garden Queen appeared before them.

"You are not the only ones in the garden. Whatever you do to the garden, you do to us all. You must be careful. Some damage can never be repaired."

Enwrapped in the race, the twins felt no shame. They reached the pole of spring neck and neck, and turned the corner, heading into summer.

Everybody watched the race on a giant screen, set in the branches of the Pavilion. Bill the Bug had gotten the screen from the Computer Mines and Phil the Gnome used his mushroom dust to deliver it quickly. Little Mark thought that the giant screen looked out of place in the nature of the Secret

Garden, but was pleased that Bill the Bug and Phil the Gnome were working together.

"They say that everything is part of the garden," said Phil the Gnome, "So this TV here, is just like a flower. It might be Freedrake's best work ever."

"Freedrake has many works," said the Garden Queen with a certain amount of pride, "His best are often his worst, and his worst are sometimes, not all bad."

They were all intent on watching the twins fly through summer. Everybody liked them both and didn't want a winner or a loser except Phil the Gnome and Bill the Bug, who argued about who was going to win.

"This is the summertime," said Bill the Bug, "This is Freedrake's time to shine. Here's where he builds his victory."

"That's what you say, robot moth," said Phil the Gnome, "But your guy better store up some energy for when it gets dark, or he's got no chance."

The racers were still in summer and Freedrake cruised ahead, the summer sun filling up the battery of his bike and speeding his lead.

"This is where I leave you behind," yelled Freedrake over his shoulder, as Weeblake began to lag in the summer heat.

The summer sun was bright and hot and both of the riders felt the effects. Freedrake's flightbike gobbled up the light and propelled him forward at a startling speed. He sped ahead of his brother, the vast groves of palm trees and cacti a blur below. While Freedrake's scooter burned the energy as fast as it came, Weeblake melted in the heat and fell far behind his brother. Weeblake hoped that his slow and steady approach would win out, so he conserved energy, hoping to make up the lost ground in future seasons. As the end of summer neared, it wasn't clear if Weeblake's strategy was working. Freedrake's lead was large, but Weeblake still surfed along comfortably, chasing his brother's bike in the distance.

At the end of the summertime, there was a strong wind blowing against both brothers. It was hard just to make it to the fall. Freedrake had charged all his batteries, but as he neared the end of the season, strong storms and headwinds blew. He was already using his reserves when he turned the corner on the autumn pole. He was ahead, but he might not have the lead he needed to win. Weeblake, still miles behind, was more tired than he thought he'd be, as he headed into fall.

Neither was prepared for what lay ahead.

The rains of autumn were strong and steady, and both brothers were soon so soaked that staying on their air ships was nearly impossible. They cast no spells and played no tricks on each other, as dealing with the nature of the garden was difficult enough. The lack of light made Malahat's flightbike slow down, so Weeblake began to catch up. To stay dry, they both ducked down into the forests of pines and cedars and spruce and maple. They dodged tree trunks and falling leaves that swirled along as they flew past. The pace of the race slowed. It was soon clear that Weeblake's strategy would probably win out. Freedrake held him off through most of the fall, but as the two neared the darkness of winter, Weeblake finally pulled ahead. They turned around the winter pole together, but Weeblake moved ahead and called to his brother over his shoulder.

"This is where I leave you behind, my brother," he yelled.

Little Mark couldn't understand why the Garden Queen would need a whole section of the garden for winter, but she assured him that the plants needed winter to grow and were alive even if they couldn't be seen underneathe all of the snow.

The Secret Garden had to have everything, and winter was a very important part of that.

Weeblake felt sure of his victory when he passed his brother, but the flying would not be easy. It was freezing cold, there was snow everywhere, and the wind was blustering. When he got to the centre of the season, he realized, there was a blizzard growing in the winter garden.

Weeblake looked back to see where his brother was but the snow was too thick for him to see. He called back, but could barely hear his own voice in the snow. He was winning the race so all he had to do was continue, but winning wouldn't mean a thing if his brother didn't finish too. He couldn't leave his brother alone in the frigid winter. Freezing and tired himself, he decided to head back into the heart of winter to find his brother. It was a blizzard with white-out conditions, but after a while, he saw his brother's flightbike crashed into a snowbank, unmoving, and getting covered up with the falling snow.

"The machine doesn't work in the darkness," Freedrake called out through the storm, "I've depleted all the energy. My batteries are empty. I haven't got any power. I need power."

Weeblake looked at him sympathetically. Even though he was exhausted himself, of course he would help his brother. He hoped his brother would do the same. In the cold of winter, he didn't have many tricks left. As a last resort, he pulled off his magician's cap, reached inside, and pulled out a rabbit.

It was Mopsy, who had escaped from the Power Plant.

"That kind of power won't work here," said Freedrake, "I need light. I need warmth. There's not enough heat here to even get me started in this blizzard. I could never win the race."

"This isn't about winning anymore, Freedrake," said Weeblake, "This is about survival. The rabbit will keep us warm."

In the coldest blizzard, in the heart of winter, the brothers were freezing. They might not make it out alive. They picked up Mopsy and held her between them, her warmth radiating into them. Their warmth shared with her warmth, and they began to weather the storm together.

And then a very strange thing happened indeed.

From the warmth of the rabbit snuggled between the two brothers, began a faint glow. The rabbit was glowing.

The warmer Mopsy got, the brighter her glow. The glow of the rabbit was faint but powerful. It was like a candle in the dark, just enough light to get a start. Freedrake kept Mopsy warm, zipped inside his coat, her light stirring them forward. Weeblake held the memory of Mopsy's warmth close to his chest as he stood up on his surfboard and willed it to float and fly. Together, they limped out of the dead of winter, slowly, one heartbeat at a time.

As they got through winter, the sunlight began to appear, making flying easier for Freedrake, but now Weeblake was exhausted. As they reached the spring pole, he collapsed on his board, and it skidded to the ground. He, too, could not finish alone. Freedrake stopped and went back to help his brother, laying him on the surfboard and placing Mopsy on his chest and then pulling him along behind his flightbike.

They rounded the corner of spring together and slowly worked their way back to the Pavilion. They landed at the base of the tree, a crumpled mess, tired, exhausted, spent. Their pointless contest had solved nothing and nearly killed them both. At least they had worked together to survive.

The faeries cheered dutifully.

Chapter Twenty

Don't Forget to Follow your Feet

The Garden Queen addressed the twins and assembled guests.

"I am happy my sons, because you have returned safely back to where you started. You now know that there are more important things than winning a silly contest. You can do much more together than alone. Apart, you are less than half of what you are together. Together, you can bring joy and prosperity to all."

Little Mark cheered loudly. This way everyone could win.

Then the Garden Queen continued.

"Now we turn to the little boy who brought us all together. He is the one we have come to love but it is time for him to go."

"Go?" said Little Mark, surprised, "I can't go. I just got here. I love it here. It's warm. It's beautiful. It's safe. I don't want to go back to the place where I get in trouble from my parents and laughed at by my brothers and sisters all the time. I want to stay."

"Little Mark, you are not of the underground," said the

Garden Queen, "You are meant to be in your world and I think you will find that your world needs you too."

"But I don't want to go. I like it here. I don't even know how to get back."

"You can go back any time that you want. And, now that your glow is gone, you can disappear naturally."

Little Mark looked down at himself and for the first time since he arrived, he could not see a glow.

"What happened?" he asked.

"Your glow has become our glow," said the Garden Queen, "Your light has become a part of our world so now you can go back to yours. As a gift, I will give you one thing. I will give you back Arthur. Arthur will be with you wherever you go in your world, though no one else will see him. What was once your biggest fear will now be your best friend. He will be your best friend, forever."

Arthur the Ex-Pet jumped up into his arms.

"So how do we get back?" asked Little Mark.

"Simple," said the Garden Queen, "Just clap your hands and imagine Auntie Mabel's garden."

Little Mark said goodbye to the Garden Queen, to Phil and Bill, to Freedrake and Weeblake, to Ai and the faeries, and to Mopsy, who didn't have to hide in Weeblake's magic hat any longer.

As he was about to go, Phil the Gnome stopped him again and said, "I'm sorry, kid."

"I understand your mischief," said Little Mark with a smile, "But you've also helped me so much."

"Yeah, well, it ain't what I did, kid. It's the show — it got a little bigger than we imagined," said Phil the Gnome.

"What do you mean?" asked Little Mark.

"You'll understand when you get back. Clap your hands

and figure it out for yourself," said Phil the Gnome, "And then, don't forget to follow your feet."

Little Mark looked at Phil the Gnome suspiciously, and then he did just that. He thought about his Auntie Mabel's garden, clapped his hands, and he was gone.

Chapter Twenty-One

Our Favourite Show

In an instant, Little Mark found himself in Auntie Mabel's Garden. He was looking down at a stone statue of Phil the Gnome where he had been when they left for the underground. Then he looked around and saw the statues of all his friends from down below and the big statue of the Garden Queen, right in the centre of the garden.

He didn't know how long he'd been gone, but he did know that he was back. He walked into his Auntie Mabel's house, and everyone looked up and began to laugh. His brother pulled out a chair for him to sit down in. They treated him like someone important and not their troublesome little brother.

"Why are you being so nice?" asked Little Mark, suspiciously.

"You've been on quite the adventure," said his mother.

"What do you mean?" asked Little Mark.

"Tell us where you've been," said his father, "Tell us what you've seen."

"We saw it too!" his brothers and sisters all screamed,

"Auntie Mabel's new computer gets all the underground television. You're number one. You're the most popular."

They turned on Auntie Mabel's new computer and on the screen were the closing credits of a show called Modern Faerie Tale. Bill the Bug and Phil the Gnome and all his friends from the underground were waving back at him from inside the computer, waving goodbye as the credits rolled.

"You were our favourite show," said his brothers and sisters.

About the Author

Patrick McGuire is an artist, writer, and grower-of-things. Born and based in Vancouver, British Columbia, Patrick is passionate about building community through permaculture, strumming his guitar, and occasionally standing on his head. This book was inspired by his garden and the creatures that live there.

Manufactured by Amazon.ca
Bolton, ON

45666120R00095